HOT SEAL, LABOR DAY

SEALs in Paradise

CYNTHIA D'ALBA

Hot SEAL, Labor Day
By Cynthia D'Alba

Cover Artist: Elle James
Editor: Delilah Devlin

CHAPTER 1

Sawyer "Nomad" Beckett roared up to the curb around the corner from McP's pub. He was lucky to have found curb parking as he hated to leave his new Harley-Davidson out of sight. It'd get its first blemish soon enough. No sense temping the gods by parking it in a crowded lot.

SEAL Team Romeo had commandeered a couple of tables behind the chained area outside the walled patio. The drinking had started without him, which he understood. Sawyer was a SEAL team floater who filled in on a temporary basis when a team had an opening. Sometimes the opening was due to illness, but occasionally a death required him to gear up and jump in. He liked the floater role. No commitment to any one team, only to the Navy.

"Nomad," Cash "Inferno" Mancini called. "Over here."

Sawyer lifted his head in acknowledgement. Carrying his helmet under his arm, he stepped over the chain and dragged a chair up to the two tables pulled together.

"Ten fucking days off," Cole "Joker" Landry said.

"I plan to spend all of them fucking," Brian "Heartbreaker" Anderson replied.

"Fuck yeah," answered Jack "Mars" Marsden.

"I think I'm taking the family on a short vacation," Chris "Zig" Bykowski added to the conversation, which drew a round of "Awws," from the team. From what Sawyer had been told, Zig had married the widow of a fallen fellow SEAL and taken on the father role with unreserved gusto.

"Gator and I are gonna hang and surf," Cash said to Sawyer. "You're welcome to join us."

"Thanks, but I've got plans."

"You guys deserve the time off," their team leader Ted "Bear" Black said. "See your families, chill, but be ready to deploy by the fifteenth."

The team had been notified this morning that they would be deployed to Niger for an undetermined length of time. While the U.S. had maintained forces all over Africa for a long period, most served in training and intelligence roles. However, there were times when U.S. forces were called upon to provide fighting support. Romeo Team was being deployed to assist in these efforts as fighting in the region had picked up.

Sawyer liked the guys of Romeo Team. If any team could tempt him to stop floating and stay, it would be this group of guys, but at this point, he would continue as he had, moving from team to team as needed. He would be deployed with Romeo as he continued to fill a spot left open with the retirement of Eli "Wolf" Miller. Team leader Ted Black had assured him that a new guy would be in place by November. Since today was the Friday of Labor Day weekend, and Sawyer had been with the team since the middle of July, he figured Ted Black was one particular sonofabitch when it came to adding a new guy to the team mix. Sawyer could appreciate that. He'd worked in a lot of different roles on a number of teams. Some were better run than others. Romeo was one of the better run teams because their leader ran a tight ship.

Sawyer had ordered three fingers of Blante's Single Barrel bourbon from a passing waitress as he'd made his way to the team. Now, the blonde returned and set his bourbon neat on the table.

"*Santé*, gentlemen," he said, lifting his glass.

Drink glasses were clinked, and the guys got back to their drinking. Sawyer leaned back in his chair and sipped the ridiculously expensive bourbon. He didn't have many vices, but sipping a high-quality bourbon was one of them.

The team stayed for only a couple of rounds of drinks. Each man seemed ready to get started on their leave. Sawyer couldn't blame them. If he had someone waiting on him, he'd probably not even shown up for drinks with the team. But he didn't, and frankly, he wasn't looking. Roots weren't his style.

He was the last man to leave because he'd wanted to slip their waitress an additional fifty-dollar tip. He fired up his Harley and roared off to his motorhome. As he traversed the streets, he racked his brain over where his motorcoach was parked. Not that he had memory problems, but he liked to move his forty-foot Winnebago around to different campsites as the mood hit him. Then he remembered he'd moved to a small, private campground on San Diego Bay, and headed there for the night. Tomorrow, he was headed to Lake Kincade for a week of doing nothing.

Originally, the plan had been to meet his parents there, but his dad, General Harold Beckett, had been ordered to Belgium for a meeting, and Sawyer's mom went wherever her husband went. It'd always been that way. He knew his parents loved him, but his dad put career first, and his mom put her husband first. Sawyer was right there in the top ten, but he was never first. He'd learned to accept it.

The Beckett family had followed Harold Beckett through every move, every promotion. In fact, at thirty-five, Sawyer had lived in more countries, cities, and states than the total number of years he'd been alive. He didn't think he'd ever started and finished a school year in the same location, but he'd adjusted. He'd had to learn to adapt if he'd wanted to survive. All those moves, all the required blending-in in new environments, all the friendships that he'd made on the fly made being a SEAL team floater ideal for him.

To say that his parents had been unhappy when he'd chosen the Navy over the Army would be like explaining the sun would be warm to the touch. Sawyer had joined immediately following high school, and now, seventeen years later, his dad kept waiting for him to realize not joining the army had been a mistake. Not going to happen.

When he got to his Winnebago, it was still early. He wasn't ready to call it a night. Lake Kincade was only three or so hours down the road. If he could change his cabin reservation to include tonight, there'd be nothing keeping him from immediately starting his vacation.

The sun had barely set when he got on the road at

seven that evening. The weather was a perfect seventy-five degrees with a light breeze. Ideal for a late evening ride on his Harley. He'd made this trip numerous times during his stay in California. The lake had some of the best trout fishing in the area.

He headed out I-15 North toward Hwy-330, which would take him to a backroad he could follow the rest of the way to Lake Kincade. The interstate was crowded, but it was a typical Friday in California. Luckily for him, the traffic was traveling at a decent pace and he reached the Hwy-330 exit in only two hours, a record for him. Being that this was Friday night of Labor Day weekend, the traffic on the highway headed to his favorite fishing lake was heavy which was why he had every intention of taking the backroad he'd discovered on one of his earlier trips.

Night had fallen when he turned onto Woodbury Road. The quarter moon gave little illumination to the dark road. This was the rural California that the rest of the U.S. never saw and would never believe existed. No streetlights to light the road. Faded divider and side lines, seen only when flashed by headlights.

Ahead of him was an older Chevrolet Malibu. The car might've been blue at some time in its life, but rust would be the better color description now. The driver was puttering along under the 50-mph speed limit, not seeming to be in much of a hurry to get anywhere. Sawyer assumed the driver was a local making his way home after work, or maybe contemplating a stop in a bar for a drink with fellow employees who had the valuable long weekend ahead. He considered the idea that the driver could be drunk, but the car was staying between the faded road striping, so probably not.

Should he roar out and pass the car? The road was

curvy with no designated passing lines. With the hills and curves added to the darkness of the evening, passing would be risky. Plus, they weren't that far outside Lake Kincade, so he'd be risking his life for what? A five or ten-minute advantage. Not worth it. He settled in behind the older car to bide his time.

The Chevy swerved, and bright red brake lights flashed. Dark smoke filled his vision. Sawyer slowed, not sure what was happening ahead. The Chevy jerked and bounced as the car eased off the road to one of the few vista pull offs.

As Sawyer passed, he noticed the blown front tire on the driver's side. He checked his rearview mirror and saw a couple of other cars pass without slowing. It was late. This was a dark, rural backroad. Stopping to help a stranger might be considered dangerous for many people.

Visitors to Lake Kincade would typically stick to the main highways, so traffic on this road would be sparce. To add to the driver's problems, cell service in the area was spotty, at best, so the driver would find it difficult to reach out to his friends and family for help. Sawyer had nowhere he had to be and no one looking for him. So, he whipped around and headed back to see if he could be of any assistance.

The Chevy sat heavily on the driver's side, listing because of the blown tire. Sawyer pulled his bike in front of the car, letting his single headlight shine on the situation. Once he got a look at the tread on the tire, he wasn't surprised to see it'd blown. The dadgum tire's tread was so past needing to be replaced, it was almost smooth.

He climbed off the motorcycle and walked up to the driver's door. The window cranked down about an inch. The aroma of fresh peaches wafted through the opening. Peaches? Odd for this time of the year.

"Need some help?" he asked.

A beautiful female with long chestnut hair looked up at him with wide eyes—wide, terrified eyes. She was gnawing on her bottom lip while her gaze whipped from him to his bike and back.

Sawyer realized he probably did look a little rough. He'd let his beard grow out during the team's last deployment so to blend in better with the male population of the Middle Eastern country where they'd been operating. His long, black hair had been whipped around during his ride, the top smashed flat by his helmet while the pieces around his shoulder were probably sticking out in all directions.

"Looks like you need a hand," he said, trying again. "Do you have a spare?"

"I don't know," she replied, still wearing her terrified expression. "My cell phone isn't working."

"Typical for this area. Pop your trunk and I'll look." He was vaguely familiar with this car. His mom had driven one like it years ago, and being the typical pre-teen male at that time, he'd spent hours looking it over.

She didn't move for a second or two, as though deciding what to do. Finally, she said, "I don't know where the latch is."

Sawyer didn't roll his eyes or do anything that would suggest he was dealing with someone whose light wasn't so bright. Instead, he smiled. "Do you have a key fob for the car? There's usually a release on it."

"Oh!" Her eyes, while still leery, brightened. "I do. Hold on." She pulled out the key and held up the fob. "Ta-da," she said triumphantly. Her thumb moved over the fob buttons until the trunk lid opened. She looked up at him with a wide grin, like she'd done something unique.

"Put on your parking brake and it'd be better if you got out of the car."

A panicked expression crossed her face.

"But you don't have to," he lied. "You're going to see me at the back passenger side blocking that tire so the car won't roll. I didn't want you to wonder what I was doing back there."

"Okay. Thanks for telling me that."

After finding a large rock and blocking the rear tire, he proceeded with pulling out the spare, which didn't look a whole lot better than the rest of the tires. He rolled the spare to the front, collected the jack from the back, and got to work. Twenty minutes later, he was pulling the large rock from under her tire.

"That should do it," he said through the one-inch opening.

"Oh, let me pay you," she said, pushing a twenty through the tiny slit.

"No, ma'am. I'm glad to help you. You keep that money." Considering the state of her car, she needed the money more than he did. "There's a tire place in the town just ahead. Why don't I follow you into Lake Kincade in case you have any more problems…? When we get there, I can show you where the tire place is, if you don't already know."

"I don't have a clue where it is." She frowned. "I doubt it'll be open this late."

"You're probably right, but you'd know where the tire store was and how to get back to it tomorrow. You're headed into Lake Kincade, right?" He'd assumed that was where she was headed, but maybe she lived outside of town. Something about her shouted that she was out of her comfort zone.

"Yes, Lake Kincade."

"Perfect. I'll pull in behind you." He grinned. "Now, don't drive too fast. I want to keep up with you," he joked.

"Oh, I won't," she said, her face so sincere he hated he'd joked with her.

They pulled back onto the road, and he followed her at a speedy forty-five for the next ten miles. Forty-five was the speed limit, and by golly, she kept that car pegged at that speed. On the downhill, as they neared the town, she slowed to forty as the speed limit sign directed.

Sawyer hated to admit it, but this was probably the slowest he'd ever gone on his bike, unless he was slowing to stop. Still, he was entertained by the obvious care the woman was giving to the twisty road. Brake lights flashed in his face so often, he wondered if there would be brakes left on that rust bucket of bolts when they got to Lake Kincade.

Once they reached the city limits, he sped up to forty-seven, passed her, and then gestured for her to follow him. There were a couple of tire places, but the closest one was Billy Bob's Tires. Corny name, but a really nice guy Sawyer had met on a previous trip.

The lights were on when they pulled in. Sawyer climbed off his bike and gestured for her to wait in her car. Billy Bob was still there chatting with an older man.

"Surprised you're still open," Sawyer said as a way of greeting.

"Got to chattin' and lost track of time. Sawyer, isn't it?"

"That's right, sir. Sawyer Beckett." He gestured to the Chevy Malibu idling in the drive. "Found this lady with a flat tire on the way into town. I put on her spare, but its tread lacks a lot to be desired. She seemed a little lost, so I don't think she lives in the area. She was kind of skittish around me." He scratched his beard. "I might look a little rough around the edges tonight."

Billy Bob chuckled. "You leave her in my hands, and I'll see what I can do."

Sawyer shook the older man's hand. "Thanks, man."

He walked back to the Chevy and gestured for the woman to lower her window. This time, she actually rolled it down halfway and he could see the woman inside. Under the fluorescent lights of the shop, he could tell her long hair was a dark shade of red and surrounded a beautiful face with a pair of jade-green eyes and a mouth with plump lips. She was a stunningly attractive woman. Too bad they were ships passing in the night.

He was intrigued by her. Where had she been headed alone so late at night? Where was her family? Her expensive linen clothes didn't fit with the ancient, rusty car. Why wasn't she driving something nicer or newer?

And why did her face look slightly familiar? Did he know her?

No, probably not, since she gave no indication that she knew him from somewhere.

She was a mystery he'd love to solve. Too bad he wouldn't get the chance.

"Billy Bob's still here. He's the older man waving from the garage. He'll see that you're taken care of."

"Thank you, again. Are you sure I can't pay you for your trouble?"

"No trouble, ma'am. You have a nice evening,"

He climbed on his Harley and headed toward Harbin's Harbor Cabins. Harbin's wasn't one of the newer, fancier places that had sprung up around Lake Kincade. The cabins had been built before Sawyer had been born, but the family-owned resort had maintained and updated them over the years. They were one of the best kept lodging secrets in the area. This was where all the locals and those in the know sent family and friends who visited.

When he got to the office, there were three envelopes taped to the door. S. Beckett, C. Kirk, and A. Cristiano.

Sawyer pulled off the one with his name and opened it knowing what he'd find. A key to his cabin—number twelve—and a welcome letter with a list of area activities. He'd requested cabin twelve, but the woman who'd made his reservation hadn't been able to guarantee a specific cabin, but had promised to make a note of his request.

Twelve was his favorite cabin. Waterfront and secluded. A place to tie off a boat if he decided to rent one, and he was leaning in that direction. A firepit for cool evenings was shared with the only other cabin in the area. Ideal. He'd have to go by the office and thank them tomorrow.

For tonight, he hauled his duffle in, took a quick shower, and hit the sheets.

Nervous energy pinged through Ana Cristiano. First the danged flat tire and now having to talk to this man about something she knew nothing about. Until about fifteen hours ago, she'd never owned a car, and wouldn't have bought this one if she could've secretly rented one. But rental cars required a credit card, which would leave a trace. Of course, so did buying a car, even from a seedy second-hand car lot. However, the owner of the dealership had been the second cousin of an acquaintance who'd vouched for him, and he'd given her a low price for cash. By the time the state processed the registration and license, maybe she will have decided what she was going to do next.

Ana did have a driver's license. Randall had taken her to get it when she'd been seventeen. In the twelve years since, she could count on her fingers and toes the number of times she'd driven, and still have toes left over.

Pulling out from the car lot had been terrifying, to put it mildly. California drivers were intimidating with their whipping around her and passing her like she was parked. A couple of times—okay, so more than five times—the passing driver had flipped her the bird. A couple of drivers had honked, making sure she saw the rude gesture. Maybe she was driving a little slower than everyone else, but she was doing the speed limit. Wasn't that what she was supposed to do?

None of that mattered. She was free. No one to clock her time. No one to tell her to watch what she ate. No one to tell her how disappointed they were. She was just Ana Cristiano, free woman, not Ana Cristiano, a woman under intense scrutiny. Watch out world. Ana was coming!

"So, I'd advise you to put on a whole new set," Billy

Bob was saying. "I can use the best of the group as your spare. But you aren't safe on these tires, ma'am. You were lucky Sawyer came by to help."

"Sawyer?"

"Sawyer Beckett, the guy who changed your tire. You didn't ask his name?" the man said, his eyebrows rising.

Ana shook her head. "I should have, but my head wasn't clicking right then. So, a full set. What will that cost?"

She thought about the cash she had on her. She had credit cards for a real emergency, but charges would show on her account and then Randall, or his son Geoffrey, would be on her doorstep as fast as he could drive.

Same issue with a check. Her bank would get the check. How long would it take for a check written in California to clear a bank in New York? She'd look that up tonight and see if she should risk it for tires.

"Welp," Billy Bob said. "I've got some good used tires off some feller's car who wanted a different brand. Lots of tread and life left in them. I can make you a good deal on those."

"Sounds perfect."

"But the wife's already called twice. This is a holiday weekend, so it'd be Tuesday before I can change them out. You gonna be in the area that long?"

She had a reservation at Harbin's Harbor for a week. The acquaintance with the second-cousin-car-salesman had recommended Harbin's. She hoped that place was better than the car.

"I plan to be. Am I safe to drive on these until then?"

Billy Bob walked around her car and looked at the

tread. "Three days. Yep, as long as you ain't got no plans to do hundred-mile sightseeing drives." He shook his head. "I wouldn't recommend it."

"Nope. I'll stay around town."

"Good."

"I've got a reservation at a place called Harbin's Harbor Cabins. Can you give me directions from here?"

Twenty minutes later, she turned onto the gravel drive that led to Harbin's. She was arriving much later than she'd told the woman on the phone when she made her reservations, and she hoped they'd held the cabin for her. Her heart sank when she saw the office light was off. In the back of her mind, she thought the girl who'd taken her reservation had said there'd be an envelope on the office door if they were closed.

To her immediate relief when she walked up to the office door, she saw a white envelope with A. Cristiano written on it. She jerked it off and looked inside. There was a cabin key—cabin number 10—and a list of area attractions. Additionally, there was a handwritten note written on the lodge map welcoming her to Harbin's Harbor, signed by the owner, Mandy.

Ana breathed a sigh of relief, the first one she'd taken since she'd planned her escape yesterday.

CHAPTER 2

Ana stretched, grabbed a pillow to hug to her chest, and rolled over to her side. Her cabin was a far superior suggestion than the car had been. She hadn't gotten a good look at the surrounding area since it'd been so dark when she'd arrived, but the small cabin was perfect. A combo living/dining/kitchenette took up one side with a bedroom and bath on the other. The inside walls were plank cedar, as were the floor and ceiling. The place smelled like lemon and cedar and was sparkling clean. Even the sheets on the bed had felt like sleeping on a cloud. There was a small porch on the front that she envisioned spending large swatches of time sitting and thinking, or maybe reading. What a luxury that'd be.

So, today was her first day of freedom in more than twenty years. What should she do with it? Not go on hundred-mile drives for sure. She'd barely gotten a chance to see the town of Lake Kincade, so maybe a walking tour was possible. On the other hand, her cabin was away from the rest of the cabins and was on the lakefront. Maybe she'd drag a chair down to the water, stick her feet in, and read a book.

Man! She sighed again. Reading a book. She couldn't remember the last time she'd read a book for pure enjoyment. Usually, Randall was shoving nonfiction books at her to *"improve her knowledge of their world and prepare her to take her place as one of the greats."* She didn't want to improve her mind. She'd gone to college, gotten the degree required, and had won a bunch of awards. Right now, she wanted some romantic fiction that'd take her away. She wanted a romantic hero to fall in love with. Randall would have a cow if he found her reading quote *such trash* unquote.

Ugh. Randall. Why did she have to think of him first thing? Way to ruin the day.

Pushing him from her thoughts, she got up, threw on a pair of linen shorts with a matching top, and made her way to the kitchen. Harbin's advertised kitchens in their cabins, and she supposed the tiny kitchenette would pass as a kitchen enough to avoid false advertising, but she sure wouldn't want to have to cook a real meal here.

She poured caffeinated coffee grounds into the drip pot and set a mug on the pot burner to let the first cup drip directly into it. She'd have hung her mouth under the black oil dripping from the grounds if that'd been possible. Having honest-to-goodness caffeinated coffee had her almost giddy. Randall only allowed her one cup of decaf coffee each day. He said her hands shook if she had any caffeine, which was a lie. He'd even restricted her from soft drinks with caffeine. She used to sneak in a Diet Mountain Dew from time to time until Randall checked the caffeine level and ruled it out of her diet.

She swapped out the mug for the pot to allow the rest of the coffee to brew. Then she carried her coffee outside to her front porch and sighed. Heaven must look like this. The blue water of Lake Kincade lapped at the nearby shore. Ripples in the waves shot diamond-like sparkles around her porch. Birds circled overhead as though looking for breakfast. Even as early as it was, boats roared up and down the lake. The Labor Day holiday weekend had begun. Let the fun begin for her, too.

Her week of freedom began with a second cup of caffeinated coffee and plopping into the front porch chair while hiking her feet upon the railing. As she sipped her second cup, much more slowly than she had her first, a Golden Retriever bounded up her stairs, its mouth wearing a smile.

"Well, hello," she said. "Aren't you a pretty girl?"

"He might prefer to be thought of as handsome," a male voice replied. "And his name is Ranger."

Ana startled, sloshing coffee over her hand. "Ouch." She set her cup on the floor and looked up. A familiar face looked back, a smile lighting up his eyes. The man who'd helped her last night.

His long, dark hair was pulled into a ponytail at the nape of his neck. The scruff on his face looked, well, scruffier than last night. His jeans bore the appearance of multiple washings, as did the soft, brown T-shirt he wore. She had to admit, the denim hugged his legs in all the right places, telling the world it was covering some thick, strong muscles. The short sleeves of the T-shirt wrapped snuggly around massive biceps. Dropping below one T-shirt sleeve band, she could make out the bottom of a tattoo. Was that an anchor?

In the morning light, he didn't look nearly as

intimidating as he had walking up to her car in the darkness last night. In fact, he sort of looked deliciously sexy.

"Oh! Hello," she said, her heart racing at an allegro tempo. "Sawyer…Sawyer…" She wracked her brain for the last name.

"Beckett," he supplied. His face broke into a wide grin. "I hope you're not the FBI agent on my case."

Her eyebrows arched. "Oh? Are you on the lam?"

He laughed. "How much more exciting would that be, but no. I'm on leave from the military."

If possible, her eyebrows rose higher. She waved her hand from high to low. "But how do you get away with the hair? The beard? I thought military guys all had buzz cuts and clean cheeks."

"Not all of us."

While they'd been talking, Ranger had walked off the porch and over to Sawyer, who crouched down to the dog's level and scratched his head and chest. The look of contentment on the dog's face made her envious. She'd never been allowed to have a dog. While she was comfortable around them, she wasn't sure of all the best canine spots for scratching. Apparently, Sawyer was in the know.

"How'd you know my name?" he asked again, not looking at her, but studying the golden-hair dog. His voice held concern, like she'd invaded his privacy or something.

"Billy Bob told me."

His shoulders visibly relaxed. "Oh, right. Was he able to take care of you?"

"He will, but his wife wanted him to head home. I'm supposed to bring the car in on Tuesday and he'll fix me up."

"You probably don't want to take that car on any long trips until then."

"Yeah, that's what he said too. No problem. I don't have to go anywhere. I can sit here and watch the boats for days. I'll be fine."

He climbed onto her porch uninvited, but that didn't seem to slow him. "Wouldn't you rather be out on the lake than just looking at it?" He swept his arm toward the water.

She leaned over to look around him—he was blocking her view after all—and then straightened. "Today? Not so much. Looks a little unsafe."

With a chuckle, he sat in her second chair, again uninvited, but she didn't mind. It was nice to have someone to talk with who didn't want to talk about music.

"Well, I'll admit there are probably some crazy drunks out there today, and maybe until Monday. But come Tuesday, if you're still here, the water will be like a sheet of glass."

She scoffed. "That'd have to be seen to be believed."

"Will you still be around on Tuesday?" His head tilted questioningly.

"Yes. You?" What she didn't add was that she'd be here as long as Randall Blagg didn't find her.

"I'm here for the week. Official leave time."

"Yeah, I'm on vacation also. Military, you said. What branch?"

"Navy. SEALs."

Her eyebrows rose in surprise. "I'm impressed."

He shrugged off her comment. "It's a job. Let's talk about you."

"Let's not," she said with a groan. "I'm on vacation, and I don't want to think about work."

"Will your family be joining you here?"

She almost laughed. Her family had no idea where she was and was most likely trying to find her without alerting the press that she was missing.

Her piano concertos booked at Louise M. Davies Symphony Hall in San Francisco for Sunday through Saturday next week would have to be canceled or rescheduled. There would be disappointed patrons, but Ana couldn't go on.

Mentally, her brain was completely fried...totally exhausted and utterly drained. She was experiencing a disconnect between her brain and her fingers. She could order herself to play a certain piece, and her hands would wait to receive instructions from her head, but nothing came. Nothing. Total silence.

Physically, she was fine, no known health issues, but her brain simply refused to tell her fingers to work. Her agent had shrugged off her pleas for a break with a promise of time off next summer. Next summer! She couldn't hold on for another year. She couldn't hold on for another week.

Ana had played a runaway fantasy game in her mind for years, never having the courage to actually do it. But during yesterday's rehearsal, her world had folded in on her like a cheap chair. Splat. Luckily, Randall hadn't been there to stop her flight. When the time had come to flee yesterday, all the information her acquaintance had provided had been invaluable.

Sawyer had asked about her family. What could they say?

Her mother, Irene Zeller Cristiano, would be wearing a furrowed brow as she paced and threatened Randall to find her daughter posthaste, while at the same time, mixing herself an extra dry martini...a little wake-me-up, she liked to call them.

Her agent, Randall Blagg, would be his usual impatient self...trying to calm her mother while snapping his fingers at his assistant.

Her father, Alexander Cristiano, would be smoking a cigar on the balcony of her parents' condo in a high-rise located in downtown Chicago on Michigan Avenue, clueless that she wasn't where she was supposed to be. Of course, the only thing he'd ever done to earn such a prestigious address was impregnate her mother.

Well, that was probably harsh on her part. He did have to put up with her grandparents, her mother's parents. That alone warranted him a lifetime of bourbon and cigars. And to be fair, he had driven her to piano lessons when her mother had had the chauffeur tied up with her errands.

What had Sawyer asked her? Oh yes. Her family.

"No, they won't be joining me. Yours?"

He shook his head. "Dad got called to Belgium for a meeting and Mom always goes where Dad goes."

She frowned in confusion. "Belgium?"

"Yeah, Dad's an Army general. Mom's a faithful military wife." He tapped his chest. "I am the ungrateful military brat who joined the wrong military branch—and I *enlisted*."

She chuckled. "Let me guess. You were supposed to be in the Army."

He tapped the end of his nose. "Only following in his footprints to West Point wasn't what I wanted to do."

"Didn't you have other siblings who could have picked up the mantle?"

"Nope. Only child. You?"

"Only child."

"I just realized I don't know your name. You must be C. Kirk or A. Cristiano." When her brows wrinkled, he said, "The other two envelopes taped to the office door."

She laughed lightly. "Ana Cristiano."

She waited for the name recognition that usually occurred when she said her name. This time, nothing. No reaction at all.

This was excellent. He had no idea who she was.

"Nice to meet you, Ana Cristiano. Do people ever pronounce your name as Anna?"

"Not if they want to live."

He laughed, a full belly howl of amusement.

"Have you had breakfast?" he asked when he finished chuckling.

She picked up her coffee cup from the porch. "Just the elixir of the gods."

"There's a great place just up the road. Pancakes. Belgian waffles. Eggs. Whatever you could want. Want to join me?"

She considered his offer, and then thought about her car. Surely the tires could go that far. Besides, they were going to a public place. No safety risk.

All her life she'd been warned about strangers and safety. Initially, because of her family's money, but now it was because of her own notoriety. Of course, in this small community, the odds of there being a fan of classical piano were slim. Hadn't she picked this place because of those odds?

"Um, can I see your ID?"

He grinned. "Smart lady." He pulled a wallet from

his front pocket and flipped out his military identification.

"Thanks," she replied.

"Don't blame you a bit," he said, slipping the wallet back into his pocket. "Lots of fake SEALs running around claiming things that aren't true."

"How infuriating that must be."

"It is. So, breakfast?"

She smiled. "Yes, that sounds lovely. We can take my car."

He chuckled. "Yeah, no. And I'm not riding in that death mobile until you get tires with some treads. You ever been on a Harley?"

Her eyes widened at the thought. Ride a motorcycle? Her mother would swoon. Her grandmother would have a case of the vapors. Randall would tell her the odds of an accident that could break all her fingers and put her career at risk.

"I haven't. It sounds exciting. Can I go like this?"

He studied her linen shorts and matching blouse. "You can if you're comfortable. Nothing in this town is what I would call classy, so anything casual is fine. Just put on shoes. You might want to change into jeans for safety, if you have some."

She glanced down at her toes and giggled. "Yeah, barefoot is a little too out there, even for me. I have a pair of sneakers and jeans. What about a helmet?" She might be mad at her agent and family, but she wasn't nuts.

"I have an extra one. Let's go."

"Give me a second to change."

She didn't want to admit how nervous she was climbing on his Harley. She'd never been on a motorcycle in all her thirty years. Her heart was pounding like a kettle drum. She was almost embarrassed by a grin so wide her cheeks hurt. Thankfully, he had the kind of Harley with an actual seat for a second rider. Sawyer handed her a purple helmet that matched his bike.

"Helmet. It's the law."

She shoved it on. "You know this is going to ruin my coiffure and yours." Her long hair was limp and stringy this morning since she'd done nothing besides drying it last night before going to bed.

He chuckled. "I'll risk it," he said as he pulled down the foot pegs for the her. "Come over to the left side. Now, swing your leg over like you're going to drive." He laughed at her wide eyes. "No, Ana, you can't drive my bike today."

She climbed on and sat in the main seat.

"Now, scoot back until you're on the back."

Once she did, he swung his leg over, righted the bike and fired up the engine.

"Ready?" he asked. "Hold on to me tight."

She nodded, tapping the front of her helmet into the back of his. Excitement raced through her veins along with a spark of nerves.

This reminded her of the first piano recital she'd given. She'd been seven at the time. Even at that age, she'd known she was good, so she hadn't been scared of the audience. She'd been excited and nervous to show what she could do. Plus, she'd been in Germany on a military base playing for military families, so if she'd messed up, no one would know. Her piano teacher at the time had said it was the ideal place to get her some playing experience. She hadn't messed up, and all the children had been given a whole day off from practice.

Sawyer revved the engine, which made the bike vibrate between her legs. That produced a very interesting tingle that bounced around her gut.

"Hang on," he shouted over his shoulder. "And don't wiggle around."

She lightly clasped hold of his T-shirt.

He shook his head. "Like this." He took her right hand and pulled it to his stomach and then did the same with her left. "And when I lean, you follow my body."

While her hands were resting on his T-shirt material, she had no difficulty feeling the firm muscles underneath. Her fingers flexed, not making an indent in the hard surface, but able to discern the groves in his abdomen. Six-pack? Eight-pack? Lord. Musicians were the only men she was around these days, and they definitely didn't sport anything like this.

She squeezed her arms a little tighter and nodded, accidentally clunking her helmet against his again. If she kept doing that, both of them would get a headache. "Sorry," she shouted. "I'm ready."

And then they were moving. She squealed with delight. Grasping her hands together, she held on with a strong hug, her front pressed firmly to his back. Gosh, he was firm, back and front. All those muscles twitched and bunched with his movements. She hadn't ever held a man like this one. Oh, she wasn't a virgin. She'd had sex at music camp when she'd been sixteen, so she knew what the male body was all about, but Sawyer's body was way beyond any male body she knew. Even looking at him was different than looking at Randall, or his son, Geoffrey. Ugh. Why did she have to think of Geoffrey Blagg?

Erasing the image of her manager and his son from

her mind, she let her gaze take in the passing land-
scape of water and boats and deep-green trees. Wind
smacked her face, and she was thankful for her
sunglasses which kept her eyes from drying out too
much.

Before she knew it, Sawyer was turning into the
gravel parking lot of DD's Diner. He pulled to a stop
and shut off the engine.

"Here we are," he said as he removed his helmet.
"The Double D. Best breakfast in town." His feet rested
on the ground as he straddled his bike.

She pulled off her helmet. "You speak from
experience?"

"I do. I've been here before. Can you get off the
back, or do you need help?"

"Can I stand on the pedal where my foot is?"

"Yep. I've got the bike."

While he kept the bike standing straight, she stood
on the foot rests and swung her leg over the low back.
Her right foot landed on the gravel and she stepped
off. "Easy peasy," she said.

He grinned as he set his kickstand and slipped off
the bike like silk flowing in the wind. So much grace.

"Grab your helmet," he said. "Wouldn't want to
lose it."

She nodded. "I wondered about someone stealing
them while we were inside."

"Probably wouldn't happen here in Lake Kincade,
but why take the chance?"

Inside, they found an empty booth. No view, but
she didn't mind all that much. Sawyer was quite the
view himself. They slid into opposite sides and
grabbed the menus that stood behind the salt and
pepper shakers.

Ana's stomach growled loudly. She slammed her hand against her belly. "Sorry."

Sawyer chuckled. "No problem. Don't be surprised if mine answers."

She laughed, glad that he didn't look as appalled as she felt. "Everything sounds so good." Her stomach took that moment to growl again. "I'm afraid we've awakened the beast who lives in my belly."

"What do you think would appease your beast?" he asked with a broad grin.

"Hmm…a waffle for sure. Maybe some bacon?" She mentally calculated the cost in her head and then the amount of cash she'd shoved into her pocket. She had enough for breakfast, but she needed to be careful. She only had a thousand to make it the rest of the week, and that included her cabin. But she'd probably put that on a credit card since it wouldn't matter by then.

"What can I get cha?" an older woman wearing a DD Diner T-shirt and shorts asked. "Can I start cha with some coffee?"

"Coffee would be great," Sawyer said. "Ana?"

She shook her head. "I'm coffeed out for today. Orange juice?"

"Be right back," the waitress said.

"What do you recommend?" Ana asked Sawyer.

He shrugged. "You really can't go wrong with anything. The waffles are good, as are the pancakes and omelets."

"What are you having?"

"DD's Big Breakfast."

Ana's gaze swept over the menu until she found it. An everything omelet, a stack of four pancakes, an order of bacon, and an order of sausage. She groaned. "I would pop if I ate all that."

"Hey, I'm a growing boy."

She laughed.

The waitress set their drinks on the table. "Ready?"

Sawyer looked at her with a raised questioning eyebrow.

"I am," Ana said. "I want the strawberry waffle, with extra strawberries, and an order of bacon crispy."

"And you?" The waitress looked at Sawyer.

"DD's Big Breakfast. Meat well cooked."

"Thanks, hon. It'll be ready in a jiff."

"So, what are your plans this week?" he asked, as he tucked their menus back into place.

Hiding, she thought, but said, "I don't know. This was sort of a spontaneous vacation. I read through what was in the envelope last night. There are so many things I could do. On the other hand, I could do nothing for an entire week and enjoy that. What about you?"

He shrugged. "Maybe rent a boat after all the crazies go home after Labor Day. There are day hikes I'd like to do, and I always enjoyed taking my bike around the lake. Thought I might do that today. Come with me. You'll enjoy seeing the lake from all the pull-off points."

She scrunched her nose. "Can I think about it?" Not that she didn't want to go. She did, so if she did, what was stopping her? Maybe it was the years of getting someone else's permission before doing anything, and wasn't she tired of that?

"Of course," he replied easily. "Now, let's talk fishing. Do you fish? You know we can fish right behind our cabins."

And just like that, their conversation veered off on

different topics. Their food came, but that only slowed their talking.

Ana dragged the last corner of waffle through the syrup on her plate and plopped it into her mouth with a sigh. "That was so good." She wiped her mouth with her paper napkin. "I am a little concerned about the extra weight I'll be bringing to your rear tire."

He laughed as he wiped his beard. "I think we'll be fine. Does that mean you'll circle the lake with me today?"

CHAPTER 3

As Sawyer waited for her reply to his invitation to ride today, he experienced an unusual feeling…nerves. Sure, he felt some nerves when he operated with a new team. Not nerves about his abilities. He knew he was solid, but he couldn't always be sure about the team. Some of them functioned like a well-oiled machine. They thought alike, worked alike, and moved as one. Some teams he'd been on had been units of men, but quietly disorganized. He hated those. Typically, he was forced to float to one of those less effective teams when someone died, something he hated. Now, Romeo Team? Bear had those guys all thinking and moving with one brain. They were the type of SEAL team he enjoyed working with, but was that enough to make him want to give up the float for permanency?

"Yes," Ana said, jerking him back to reality.

"Yes? As in, you want to go around the lake?"

She smiled, and his heart tripped over. He doubted she had any idea how beautiful and sexy she was.

"Yep. Around the lake."

"Great. It's a long drive, and it could get cool before we get back. Do you have a jacket at your cabin?"

"No, sorry." Her face fell.

"No problem. I have one you can wear, if you don't mind it being a little big."

"I don't mind."

"Perfect. Let me settle the bill, and we'll head back to my cabin to grab my jacket."

She pulled a twenty from her pocket. "This will cover mine."

He looked at her twenty and frowned. "Put that back in your pocket. I've got this."

"But—"

"But nothing. I invited you. I'm paying." He slid from the booth. "And that's final."

"Fine, but you'll let me pay for dinner, maybe?"

"Sounds like a deal." Oh, hell, yeah. He'd let her pay, or at least say he would. That'd give him more time with her, something he definitely wanted.

Back outside, she put on his helmet, and climbed on his bike like she'd done it a million times. The view of her on his bike was, well, better than any dream he'd ever had. But, for the life of him, he couldn't remember why her face and name were so familiar. It'd come to him eventually.

After a quick stop for his jacket—her arms were so delicate that his jacket would provide a extra layer in case of an accident…not that he expected one—he roared out of Harbin's Harbor Cabins. Behind him, Ana's breasts were firmly pressed into his back, as they had been during the ride to the diner. As before, her arms wrapped snuggly around his waist. He could hear her laughter as they rode out of town toward Lakefront Circle.

Lakefront Circle had a deceiving name. While it was a road that circled Lake Kincade, there were numerous spurs off of it that led to housing developments and viewpoints that were on the lakefront. If he got on Lakefront and never stopped, just drove the loop, it would take a couple of hours. However, if he pulled down any spur, or stopped for views, he could easily kill the entire afternoon, which was exactly what he had planned.

His original plan had been to meet his parents here. Lake Kincade was close to Coronado. He'd been here before and had enjoyed the small town's personality. When they had to cancel, he considered not coming, but he'd been on his own for years, and alone for most of those. Traveling solo was his usual *modius operandi*, so another vacation alone wasn't that upsetting.

That's not to say he hadn't had girlfriends he'd taken away for weekend getaways. He had, and could have more if he wanted, but he hadn't met a woman he felt any spark for or any real connection to until this week. Ana Cristiano had changed that for him.

The first glimpse of her face last night had rocked him back on his heels. It'd been her eyes looking at him through a half-opened window. A deep jade green that had bored a hole into his chest.

However, this morning...wow. He'd gotten a look at the entire package while she'd been petting Ranger. Her hair was a rich, deep auburn that tumbled over her shoulders and down her back in waves. He hadn't realized how large her eyes were last night. Today, her large eyes with her long, dark eyelashes, her straight nose, and full red lips made an image impossible to ignore. She was a knock-out, or at least she knocked the breath from his lungs.

Instead of Lakefront Circle, he made an impromptu decision to ride to the top of the mountain first to give her an overview of the area. He turned on Mountain View Drive and started the climb. After about fifteen minutes, he turned onto a dirt and gravel road that passed between arching trees. If someone didn't know it was here, the turn could be easily missed.

"Where are we going?" Ana asked.

"Up the mountain. Special viewing area. Trust me." But he could hear the slight hesitation in her voice. What an idiot he was. Of course, she'd been nervous. He'd told her one thing and was doing completely something else. Any woman would be anxious to be on the back of a bike with a man she'd just met who was taking her somewhere other than what he'd said.

He rode into an open area with large boulders blocking the drop down the mountain. She climbed off the bike almost the second he stopped.

She whipped off her helmet. "Where are we?" she asked, her gaze whipping around.

"I'm sorry," he said. "I'm so used to doing whatever comes to mind. Honestly, so sorry. I thought you might enjoy the view from the top of the mountain before we circle the lake. That way, you have an idea of where we are. I didn't mean to frighten you."

"I'm not frightened." She tossed her hair over her shoulders. "I'm just not big on surprises."

He drew in a deep breath and nodded. "Got it. No surprises. But again, I'm sorry. Dumb move. I promise to tell you before I go off-script."

With a nod, she said, "Okay, now, what did you want me to see?"

They stepped over to the large boulders, and he pointed out various areas.

"See that black road that circles the lake? Well… sort of circles it. That's Lakefront Circle." He pointed west. "Over there is the chairlift that takes riders up to a downhill sled ride. No snow needed." He looked at her. "I think you would enjoy that. Also in that area are go-karts and miniature golf." He pointed a little more west. "That's where we are staying."

She leaned out to look. "I see it." She turned to him. "I'm so glad not to have ended up in some impersonal hotel. I lucked out with my cabin."

"You must've booked it a long time ago. Harbin's Harbor books up months in advance because of demand."

Shaking her head, she said, "I didn't. I literally called yesterday and got lucky. There was a last-minute cancellation."

His mouth stretched into a grin. "Right. I cancelled my parents' cabin. You must've gotten it."

Mentally, he thanked his parents for cancelling. That explained how the two of them had ended up with the two cabins away from everyone else.

"That's right. You said your parents had to go to…"

"Belgium."

"Right. Beautiful country. You ever been there?"

"I have. Being in a military family, we traveled a lot. We were based in Germany for a number of years, so Mom and I would venture out to visit other countries when Dad was busy. I think I've been to most of the European countries."

"Me, too." Her voice reflected the smile on her face.

"When was the first time you went?"

She tapped a finger on her lip as she thought. The tapping drew his attention from her face directly to her luscious lips. What would they taste like? Would they feel as cushiony as they looked? She licked her lips.

Fuck. His brain swirled off in directions it didn't need to be dancing off to!

"I think I was about seven? Or maybe eight."

What was she talking about? He was thinking kisses, and she was talking about…Oh yeah. Traveling.

"I bet you had fun with your parents."

She shrugged. "Not really. My mom didn't go, and Dad spent most of his time exploring Germany. At that point, Randall wasn't my manager and was more interested in pushing Geoffrey." Her face brightened. "But I had fun, just not with Dad. I met a bunch of the kids who lived on the base and played in the snow."

"Oh yeah, we used to have tons of snow, which is probably why I live in California now."

With a chuckled, she said, "I love snow, but I love it most when I don't have to leave the house." She wrinkled her nose. "If I have to go somewhere, give me warm weather, clear skies, and dry roads."

"Amen. Ready to head on?"

"Sure. Where to next?" Her eyebrow lifted.

He chuckled. "No surprises. I thought we'd head to the very top of the mountain for more views, and then head back down the way we came. If we go over the mountain, we'll move away from Lake Kincade. Once we get back in town, let's grab sandwiches and find somewhere to picnic along the drive."

She groaned. "Lunch? We just ate breakfast."

"Not hardly. That was a couple of hours ago."

Her eyes popped wide. "Wow. Where did time go? Okay, that sounds like a plan. Let's ride."

He grinned. "At your command."

The top of the mountain took about twenty minutes because of the switchbacks. At the top, he parked in another area with large boulders blocking the mountain drop, but this time, they weren't alone. Six other cars were already parked. People spilled out in all directions.

He pointed to the empty boulder on the right. "Let's head over there."

"Will the view be as good as trying to wiggle into the crowd in the center?"

"Probably not, but we can always come back later in the week if you want. Holiday weekends brings out all the tourists." He emphasized the last word with a self-deprecating sneer, which made her laugh and made his heart soar. He loved hearing her laugh.

Still, they walked over to the last boulder, and Ana climbed on top and sat. She bent one leg and wrapped her arms around her knee.

"I love this view." She grinned at him. "Even from way over here."

He leaned on the boulder and looked over the vista. "Me, too. Don't get me wrong. Living on the beach is great, too, but I love mountain air."

"You live on the beach?"

He chuckled. "At times. I have a motorhome. Sometimes, when training has had me in sand and salt water for days, I want to get away from all of it. I take the motorhome and move to an RV park inland. When I get tired of that view, I move to a different park."

A deep frown creased her brow. "Doesn't all the

moving get tiring? Or better yet, do you ever forget where you parked?"

Chuckling, he said, "Moving is pretty easy. Unplug electric, pull up hoses, hook my truck to the RV for towing, my bike secured in the truck bed, and pull out. Occasionally, I have to think about where home is, but I always remember." He tapped his head. "I have a secret way to remember."

She leaned forward. "Oh, tell me."

"But then it wouldn't be a secret."

She laughed. "I suppose you're right." She turned to look at the view. "Lake Kincade is bigger than I thought it would be. How big is it? Do you know?"

From where he leaned next to her, a sweet floral scent tickled his senses. He leaned closer, as though he was being pulled by a string. No string, however. Just the most interesting woman he'd met in a long time.

"Size? About twenty-thousand acres, I think. It can fluctuate according to snow fall." He pointed to a mountain in the distance. "Can you see the ski slopes?"

"I can." She looked at him. "Have you ever been here in the winter to ski?"

"Sure."

"Black diamond sort of guy?"

He arched an eyebrow in answer.

"Got it. No bunny slopes for you."

He laughed. "What about you?"

She got a sheepish look on her face. "Randall won't let me."

"Who is Randall? You've mentioned him before. You're not married, right?"

She fake-gagged. "Married to Randall? Kill me now. No, Randall is my manager."

"Manager?" He frowned. "Why do you need a manager?"

Sighing, she said, "He manages my career."

"And that would be?"

"I play the piano."

His mouth quirked. "Hmm. Would you have played with any bands I might recognize?"

She shook her head. "Doubt it," she said with another sigh.

"Are you any good?"

"Yeah, I'm pretty good."

"Interesting." He didn't play an instrument of any kind, not that that had stopped his mother from paying for lessons on the guitar, the trumpet, and the drums. He sucked at all of them.

"Ready to head to circle the lake?" she asked.

He picked up on her obvious change of subject. "Sure."

"How long is the drive?"

"A couple of hours, but if we stop for lunch like we talked about, we'll probably waste most of the afternoon. I'm sorry. I didn't ask if you had other plans or needed to be back at a certain time."

"No plans. Let's go, easy rider."

By the time they got down the mountain and back to the town of Lake Kincade, it was close to noon. The sun was high in the sky. Holiday traffic was brutal. Bumper to bumper traffic lined the road through the center of town. He suspected the traffic on the road ringing Lake Kincade would be much of the same.

"Maybe driving Lakefront circle isn't such a good idea," he said. "I keep forgetting the Labor Day crowds." He pulled into the lane of slow traffic.

"The road traffic looks worse than the boat traffic

on the lake, and I didn't think anything could look worse than that."

"Want to do this another day? I promise that everyone will disappear late Monday."

"Probably the best plan."

He heard her sigh. He hoped that meant she was as disappointed as he was. He turned into a grocery store parking lot and parked.

"Let's get some stuff and cook out tonight for dinner. We have a great firepit. There's a grate that goes over it. Maybe we could grill some steaks."

"Or hot dogs," she said gleefully. "I never get to eat hot dogs. Steaks I have all the time. I want some serious taboo foods."

He laughed. "Taboo foods. I love it. Well, come on and pick up something really terrible for dinner."

After the stop at the store, where he let Ana pick all the ingredients for tonight's meal as well as a couple of sandwiches for lunch, they climbed back on the bike and headed back to Harbin's. He parked his motorcycle beside her car, and eyed it. Yeah, she probably did play the piano, but from the looks of her car, she wasn't making much money from her gigs. Later, he'd look her up online and check out the bands she'd played with. His taste in music ran toward country, but he doubted that was her forte. Still, it'd be cool if he could mention some of her previous band gigs tonight. In the meantime, he'd make sure to pick up any expenses. Heck, this cabin was probably putting a serious dent in her money.

"I forgot to ask you if you wanted some wine or something," he said.

She shrugged. "I don't know. Which wine pairs well with hot dogs, chips, and s'mores?"

He laughed. "Beer."

"Great. I'll have a beer with dinner."

Narrowing his eyes, he asked, "Have you ever had a beer?"

She scoffed. "Of course."

He doubted her, but he couldn't say why. He knew they were probably close in age, but she came off as someone who'd lived a much more sheltered life.

"Okay, then. I'm going to run and grab some beers to ice down."

"And I'm going to sit on my porch and read a book."

When he got back, she was on her porch as she'd said she'd be, a paperback book clutched in her hands.

"Good book?" he asked as he walked past her cabin on the way to his.

"Shh. The heroine is walking down a flight of stairs into a basement looking for the serial killer." She never lifted her gaze off the page.

He walked on, chuckling to himself.

The sun began dropping in the sky about six-thirty. He'd set up the firepit with wood and found some hangers to use for roasting the hot dogs and the marshmallows. None of that had taken long. What ate up his afternoon had been his internet research, and what he'd found stunned him to his core.

Ana had been correct when she'd said he'd never heard of any of the *quote* bands *unquote* she'd played with. She played with orchestras, not bands, and who hadn't heard of the San Diego Philharmonic Orchestra? He remembered sitting through a performance of the Vienna Philharmonic Orchestra when he'd been about ten. Talk about misery. He had begged to go see Destiny's Child or The Rolling Stones, but his mother had been sure the culture would be good for him. At ten, he'd been too young to appreciate all the talented musicians.

However, that afternoon, he must have watched twenty different videos of Ana playing with various orchestras. In every case, she'd been the star attraction. They were her back-up. Never had he experienced anything like the feelings Ana's music produced. He'd been sucker-punched by the degree of her talent.

So, why was she here in some tiny cabin in Lake Kincade, and why was she driving that rust bucket in the parking lot?

And should he blow her cover and let her know he knew who she was, or continue to accept the person she wanted him to see?

CHAPTER 4

A na's heart raced as her breathing labored. The pages in her book stuck to her sweaty fingers. The heroine was in so much trouble. The bad guy had her trapped below ground, and her lover, the town's sheriff, didn't know where she was. She was the only person who realized the town doctor was the serial killer and now she was in his grasp.

Ana turned the page and—

"Ready for a beer?"

She screamed and chunked the book toward the voice. Sawyer chuckled, catching the book before it hit his forehead.

"Ohmygod," she said, pressing her hand to her chest where her heart was beating a million times a minute. "You scared the bejesus out of me."

"Bejesus?" He laughed and climbed onto her porch. "I haven't heard that word in a long time."

"My grandmother, my dad's mother, used to say that when I would jump out from behind the couch and surprise her." She grinned and took the bottle of beer he offered. "Now I know how she must have felt. My heart almost jumped out of my chest," she said with a laugh. She hoped this beer tasted better than the last time she'd tried to drink one. But it sounded so pretentious to ask for wine, or at least she thought so.

"Good book, huh?"

"So good, and scary."

"Scary, huh? I might have to skip it. Could give me nightmares," he said with a wink.

"Right. Big, strong SEAL having nightmares from a book."

He straightened and puffed out his chest. "Big and strong, huh? What about good-looking and sexy?"

She rolled her eyes. "Like you don't own a mirror," she said with a scoff.

He laughed as he pretended to fluff his hair. "So, you read all afternoon?"

"It was wonderful, but maybe I might need to read something less suspenseful. The idea is relaxation."

Gesturing toward her beer with his, he said, "*Santé*," and tapped his beer to hers.

"*Santé*." She took a little sip and fought the grimace that wanted to make itself known. Surely if she drank enough, she'd get used to the taste. "Do you speak French?" she asked, trying to deflect the conversation away from the beer.

"*Oui*." He shrugged. "*Pas bien*."

"Not well? I suspect you're being modest."

"I do okay. I mean, I get around France without too many sneers."

She laughed. "That alone is a feat. Any others?"

"*Sí, pero de nuevo no bien*."

"But I bet you can order a beer in Mexico without a problem."

"*Sí. Cerveza, por favor.* And even more important is *dónde está el baño?*"

She laughed. "Yes, I agree that knowing where the bathroom is located is important after drinking lots of beer."

He grinned. "You speak French and Spanish?"

"A little of both, enough to order a meal."

"Any others?"

She shrugged and glanced down. Her parents had always told her that bragging was vulgar. Her reply came hesitantly. "Some. A little Portuguese, some Italian, some German, but I totally suck at Russian."

He leaned back in his chair with a whistle. "I can't decide if I'm impressed or intimidated."

"Don't be either. You said you traveled as a kid. You know how you pick up things as a kid." She lifted one shoulder. "That's how it was for me. After a few different languages, new ones come easier. Now, when are we starting the fire?"

"Do I have a pyromaniac as a neighbor?"

She grinned. "Guilty, but I can totally control the urges." She held up two fingers. "I swear. You can check. No buildings burned down."

No buildings, but she was in the process of burning down her relationship with Randall and her parents. She didn't give a flip about Geoffrey one way or the other, which might distress those around her trying to convince her that Geoffrey was her future.

"Something wrong with your beer?" he asked.

"What? Oh, umm, no. It's great." She took another sip.

He shook his head. "Woman, confess. You're not a beer drinker."

Her shoulders slumped. "But I want to be."

He laughed. "Tell you what. We'll get the fire going, and while you watch it, I'll get the red wine from my cabin I bought for you."

Her mouth gaped.

"Yeah, I figured you'd be relieved."

With a smile, she saluted. "Pyromaniac reporting for duty, sir."

The rest of the evening seemed to fly by. Of course, the passage to time was helped by the bottle of excellent merlot he'd bought for her.

She discovered she liked her hot dog skins crispy and her marshmallows slightly brown. S'mores were the best dessert she'd ever had.

As she licked her fingers after her third s'more, she said with a sigh, "I think I'm in love."

Sawyer patted his chest. "With me? Love at first sight?"

She laughed. "I think you mean, love at first bite." She licked the sticky marshmallow off the fingers of her other hand. "I don't know where this bad boy has been all my life."

He chuckled. "Girl scout camp?"

"Nope. Never went. I did go to music camp when I was sixteen, but the meals were catered, and no desserts were allowed."

With a grimace, he said, "Sounds horrible."

She thought about that summer. She'd met Joey Collins at camp. He was there for the trumpet, she for piano. He had great lips, probably from blowing on that horn for hours at a time. She'd had sex with Joey while they'd been at camp. It'd been okay, but she'd failed to see what all the hype was about. They'd promised to stay in touch, but they hadn't, and she didn't think either of them had cared that much about that.

She smiled. "Some parts were better than others."

He studied her face for a moment and then smiled. "Music camp sex."

Her mouth dropped. "W….what?" Her shoulders drew back, and she sat up straighter. With a sniff, she said, "I have no idea what you mean."

He roared with laughter. "You most certainly do." He leaned in as though they were passing secrets. "What was his name?" he whispered. "I promise I'll never tell."

She groaned. "Joey."

He snorted. "Joey? Not Joe? What kind of teen still goes by Joey?"

"He was a good trumpet player."

Sawyer laughed again. "Great lips, am I right?"

Dropping her head back on her shoulders, she groaned again. "Get out of my head."

His grin said he was enjoying this way too much.

"Fine then," she said. "Who was your first?"

"Julie Baker," he said with a sigh. "What a woman."

"If she's so great, why aren't you with her?"

"Well, I was fourteen, and she was eighteen and leaving for college. She blew me off for older guys," he said with disgust. "Can you image? Dumping all this prime flesh for a college man."

She laughed. "Bet she'd be sorry today."

"So, we're back to talking about my sexiness and devastatingly good looks?"

With a snort, she said, "And we've come full circle. I think that means it's time for me to leave so you can be alone with yourself."

She stood. He grasped her hand.

"Thank you for one of my best days in a while," he said.

She smiled at him. "Me, too."

"Tomorrow?" His eyes were questioning.

Did she want to spend the day with him tomorrow, too? Heck, yeah, but maybe she needed to stick a little pin in his ego.

"I don't know," she said, making her voice sound hesitant. "I do have that book to read."

He lifted an eyebrow. She'd seen that before, and darn if it wasn't cute.

She rolled her eyes. "Okay, okay. What's the plan?"

"I know you hate surprises, but you liked the red wine surprise, right? It's Sunday, so maybe the tourists will sleep in a little. I know something I think you would enjoy. Trust me?"

First, the disdain in his voice when he said tourists cracked her up. Second, did she trust someone she'd only known a day? Why did she feel like she could?

She blew out a long and loud sigh. "Fine. I'll trust you, but…" She narrowed her eyes threateningly. "You're on probation. We'll see how you do."

He placed a light kiss on her knuckles. "See you tomorrow. Seven, if you want breakfast."

"Seven, it is. Night."

"Night."

Ana headed inside her cabin, shocked to see that it was close to ten-thirty. Not that ten-thirty was all that late, but they'd lit the fire a little after six. Those hours had seemed like minutes.

Tomorrow was another day of freedom, and one more day closer to her thirtieth birthday. Would she have a clue what to do by then?

THE NEXT MORNING, ANA WAS ON HER PORCH BY SIX a.m, strong and caffeinated—because who was going to tell her she couldn't?—coffee perched on her chair arm beside her elbow. The lake show, i.e., crazy boaters and jet skis, were already zooming up and down in front of her. For a large lake, her little area sure seemed to get a lot of traffic. As she watched, a boat pulling a couple of young kids on a large towable innertube passed in front. The kids' screams and laughs echoed off the lake, pulling a smile to her mouth.

Her parents, and then Randall, would never have allowed her to do something like that. She could break a finger, or even an arm, and then what? Other than the month she'd spent at music camp, she'd rarely been left alone to make her own decisions. It had occurred to her that sex with Joey Collins had been more about striking out at all her restrictions more than lust-driven passion.

But she'd gotten that pesky virginity thing behind her, not that she'd used that freedom very much. A couple of times in college—again making her wonder what was the big deal about sex? When she read romance novels, the heroine was always having screaming orgasms. She had been mainly glad to have the deed done and over so she could get back to her piano.

Once she'd gotten through her doctorate in music, she'd hit a serious sexual dry spell…like her vagina was probably dusty. She was chuckling at the thought when she heard Sawyer's cabin door slam.

49

"Morning," he called, his voice all strong and cheerful.

How could people be happy and peppy in the morning? It wasn't natural. She'd actually gotten up early so she could pour a couple of cups of coffee in her before she had to deal with people. If she was this grumpy with caffeine, she knew she had to be worse without it. Suddenly she felt bad about all those early morning rehearsals when she might have been a tad touchy.

She lifted her coffee mug in a salute. "Getting my caffeine. Trust me, you want me caffeinated up."

He chuckled and joined her on the porch. He carried his own mug. "I understand," he said, tapping his mug to hers. "How's the show?" He tipped his head toward the lake.

"Entertaining."

"You ever waterskied?"

"I've never been on a small boat. I've been on a large liner, even a yacht or two, but nothing like I'm seeing in front of us."

"That settles it. We're taking a boat out. Do you swim?"

She scoffed. "Of course, I swim."

"Good, but I'm a pretty good life guard." He waggled his eyebrows. "You know, in case you almost drown and need mouth-to-mouth."

She looked at him and then made a dramatic roll of her eyes, which made him snort.

"So, what's on the agenda today?"

"Up a mountain."

"But…" She frowned. "Didn't you just say we'd get a boat?"

He nodded. "Yep, but…" He tilted his head toward

Lake Kincade. "Traffic today will be crazy. Check the waves. A boat ride will be choppy and rough. By Tuesday or Wednesday, the lake will be calmer with fewer boats, and a boat ride much more enjoyable. But if you want to head out today...?"

"I'd rather wait until we have the lake to ourselves."

He chuckled. "Well, not exactly to ourselves. Now about the mountain..."

"Didn't we do the mountain yesterday?"

"Ah, yes, but different mountain, and..." He added when she opened her mouth to speak. "And, this one has activities to do. It'll be crowded, so we'll need, or at least *I'll* need, to wear my coat of patience."

"Coat of patience, huh? Do you get easily impatient?"

He smiled. "Not really. I've had to fit in and adapt to so many new schools, locations, and teams, I've gotten pretty good at it."

"Teams? I don't understand."

"SEAL teams."

"Excuse my denseness, but why do you have to adapt to a bunch of different teams? Maybe too much television, but don't SEALs get on a team and stay there?" She hoped it wasn't because no one liked him or could work with him. That would definitely affect her opinion of him, which was quite high at the moment.

"I'm a Navy SEAL floater. That means, I fill in when a team needs an extra man. Sometimes, guys retire and the team leader is looking for just the right guy. That's where I am now. Sadly, sometimes a SEAL does die on duty, but his responsibilities still have to be fulfilled. So, I go where I'm needed."

"Do you like that? Sounds lonely."

He shrugged. "It works for me. When will you be ready to go?"

She noted his abrupt change of subject. Rather than try to dig out more information about his job, she said, "Ready." She wiggled her toes. "Just have to get some shoes. Jeans okay for today?"

"Yes, ma'am. Perfect."

"Bike, or are we taking my car?"

He sighed. "Your car is a deathtrap."

"It is not," she said indigently. "She just needs a little love to make her shine."

"Love? How about paint and new tires? Does the radio even work?"

Warmth climbed her neck, and she was sure her cheeks were red. "It works...sort of."

His eyebrows arched. "Sort of? What does that mean?"

"I get AM, okay?"

He threw his head back with a deep laugh. "AM? I didn't even know there were still AM stations."

She joined his laughing. "There's not much, but if you love gospel music, preaching, and right-wing conspiracies, I've got you covered."

"Oh, lord," he said, still laughing. "Fine. We'll take your car since we're only going a few miles, but I'm driving."

"Fine," she said with a shrug. "But don't hurt my baby."

He was still laughing when she went inside to get her shoes.

Sawyer promised her breakfast when they got to the top of the mountain. That promise was the only reason she let him drive past DD's Diner. She'd been craving waffles.

He hadn't been wrong about the short drive. A couple of miles past the diner, he pulled into a lot at the base of the mountain. Climbing the mountain directly in front of the car was a chairlift, chair after chair going up the side.

"Are we getting on that?" she asked, pointing to the chairlift.

"Yep. All the way up."

She gulped.

"Are you scared of heights?" His face was full of concern. "I mean, I didn't even think about that. If you are, I mean, we can do something else."

"Oh, no, no," she said, pushing a heavy dose of gaiety into her voice. "Not a problem. Not a problem at all."

"Have you been on a chairlift before?"

"No, but it looks like a grand adventure."

He studied her face. She smiled broadly like one does when one is boldface lying. Well, she wasn't exactly lying. She'd never had a problem on a plane, and those were high in the air, right? Surely a few feet off the ground couldn't be worse, right?

"Okay, then. Let's do this."

He bought their tickets and held her hand as they stood in line for the lift. As the chairs entered the terminal, people stepped in front of the oncoming seat and were swept off their feet and up into the air. She suspected her hand was sweaty, because her heart raced with nerves.

Then, too soon, it was their turn to load on the lift.

Sawyer led over to the platform. "Our chair is coming. Bend your knees a little."

She did.

"Perfect," he said. "Now, let the chair scoop under your butt."

The edge of the wooden seat bumped her thighs, causing her to sit.

"That's it," he said with a wide grin. "You did it."

Sawyer lowered a metal bar across their laps, she assumed to keep them from falling out.

She looked down as the earth moved away. She'd been wrong, wrong, wrong. Legs dangling out of a chair a million feet off the ground while it races up the side of a mountain was so much worse than being on a plane.

"How long does this take?" Her voice was a little shaky

Sawyer looked over at her and held out his hand, palm up. "Want to hang on to something?"

"Yes," she exclaimed and grabbed his hand. "Do we ride this back down?"

"We can, but there's another way to come down."

"In a car?"

He laughed and squeezed her fingers. "I won't let anything happen to you, Ana Cristiano."

They rode for a couple of minutes and then he asked, "I was thinking last night about something you said. You were in Germany when you were about seven, right?"

She nodded, her voice deciding it wasn't needed, unless she wanted to scream, and then it'd be all over that.

"How old are you now?"

She swallowed. "Trying to distract me? That's nice, but—"

"Nope. Age. Cough it up."

With a chuckle, she said, "I'll be thirty on Thursday."

He turned slightly in the chair to look at her.

"Be careful," she demanded. "You have the car keys. If you fall off, how will I get home?"

That made him gasp with laughter. "Oh, Ana. You are a funny one. We have to do something special on Thursday for sure. What's your favorite birthday celebration? We'll do that."

"Umm, I don't have a favorite birthday celebration. Usually, I have to play those nights."

Like every other night of her life. If a group of people jumped out and yelled "Surprise," she'd probably have a stroke and die on the spot.

"Well, that's awful. I suggest we plan something awesome and totally unforgettable that day, right?"

She smiled. "That sound's nice."

"Nice? Hell, woman, it's your birthday. I don't do nice. I do memorable. And look, we made it to the top."

Ana swung her head away from his handsome face. "Hey. That wasn't bad at all. Told you I wasn't afraid of heights."

He chuckled. "Right. When we get to the landing, we stand, and hurry down the ramp out of the way of the next chair. The lift is made for snow skiers, so they just glide down the ramp on skis. We get to run."

"I can do that. Tell me when."

"Just keep holding my hand and follow my lead."

She liked holding his hand. His fingers were thick and a little callused. Her thin fingers felt safe and protected surrounded by his.

They neared the ramp. The chair safety bar lifted.

"Now," he said, and pulled her out of the chair.

They raced down the ramp, him grinning and her laughing like a loon.

"You did it," he said. "Never had a doubt."

"I might have had one or two," she said with a grin. "Now, food. My tummy demands food."

She noticed he didn't drop her hand as he led them to a log building with the word *EATS* above the door. "Eats? Really?"

"I know. Corny as crap, but good eats."

She giggled. "You haven't led me wrong yet, so lead on."

He waggled his eyebrows. "Just give me time."

They hurried to the last empty table for two and collapsed into chairs.

"Whew. I was worried I wasn't going to beat that old couple trying to get this table," he said with a broad smile. "I guess we're lucky she was using a cane."

Ana laughed and punched his arm. "You are so bad. There wasn't any old couple."

"Not right now, but I guarantee we'll run into plenty today."

They ordered coffee and juice while they each studied the large chalkboard hanging on the wall with the day's specials. With relief, she saw a pecan waffle with warm maple syrup as one of the choices.

"Let me guess," he said. "Pecan waffle with warm syrup and an order of crisp bacon."

She smiled innocently. "It's like you're a mind reader."

He buffed his nails on his shirt. "What can I say? Too many smarts for my own good."

She rolled her eyes then chuckled. She realized she hadn't laughed or chuckled or, heaven forbid, giggled in a long time. Sawyer Beckett was good for her soul.

Breakfast was as delicious, and filling, as DD's Diner had been.

As they exited the restaurant, she patted her belly. "I'm stuffed."

"But happy?"

"Oh, yeah. So very happy."

He took her hand again and they walked around the area. "In the winter, this is filled with skiers, snow depending, of course. But in the summer months, I've seen lots of families up here." He pointed. "Miniature golf over there." He gestured to the right. "There's go-karts over there. Behind those, there's a ropes course, but I'm thinking that isn't your thing."

"I know what a ropes course is, and I'll pass, *thankyouverymuch.* But don't let me slow you down. Feel free to jungle climb and walk skinny ropes from tree to tree."

He grinned. "Too much like my day job. I'll pass. There's also a zipline where they pull you up a line and you get to zip back down."

She looked at him with a raised eyebrow and an upturned lip. "Seriously?"

He laughed. "I thought you might skip, but honestly, it's not bad and kind of fun."

"Isn't that like your day job again?"

"Yes, but it's one of the best parts. Nothing like rappelling out of a helicopter."

"I'll pass. Next?"

He grinned. "Well, there is the alpine slide, which is okay for kids ages five and up."

"I could probably handle that."

"And last, but the best thing up here is—"

"Wait. Let me guess. Some type of ride that goes really fast."

"A mountain gravity-controlled roller coaster, and before you say, 'No way' the rider can control the speed. Slow down. Speed up. Whatever you want."

"Hmm. Maybe. Can we work our way up to that?"

"Miniature golf, it is."

Through the whole discussion and his pointing, he never let go of her hand. She found she didn't mind that. In fact, she might have liked it.

At miniature golf, they got in line behind a senior couple, only the man was using the cane instead of the woman. Sawyer elbowed her and nodded his head toward the couple.

"I was close," he whispered in the ear.

His warm breath tickled her ear and sent chills down her back. She didn't reply because she was too busy trying to tame her shivers.

Two putters and two balls later—purple for him and pink for her—they stepped up to the first hole.

"I should warn you that I almost went pro," she said, putting an extremely serious expression on her face.

"Really? Instead of piano?"

She shrugged. "It was seriously a toss-up." She lifted her hands and raised the right one. "Golf?" Then she lowered it and raised the left. "Piano?"

He chuckled. "Good thing we don't have a bet on this match. I'd hate to lose my entire paycheck to a hustler."

She grinned. "Ladies, first."

He scoffed. "Of course."

She tapped the golf ball, and fate smiled on her. The first hole required she pass the ball under a bear who straddled the path to the hole. Once past him, the hole was straight ahead. Her pink ball rolled very slowly through the bear's legs and out. She raced to the end to see what would happen. When her ball got to the hole, it sat there for a couple of seconds before it dropped into the cup.

With a shout, she jumped. "Hole-in-one," she announced, as if she'd performed some fabulous feat.

"I see that," he said with a smile. "Now, I'm all nervous and shit."

She laughed.

Sawyer's purple ball flew past the bear and the hole, bouncing off the rear board and coming to a stop about four inches from the cup. He tapped it in.

Pulling the score card from his hip, he said, "Let's see, two pars, right?"

"Ha, ha. That's a sad par for you and a rocking birdie for me."

They continued the game, the lead swinging back and forth between them. She suspected, but would never be able to prove, that he was letting her win. Fine. She had no problem kicking a SEAL's ass.

In fact, on the sixteenth hole, she set her ball down and looked at him. "If you're letting me win, that's fine. I will have no guilty conscience about humiliating you on this course."

"Oh, baby. That was the wrong thing to say." His eyes narrowed. "The gauntlet has been thrown down. Prepare to lose."

She looked at the windmill turning in front of her. Yeah, this would be a challenge. The timing had to be perfect or her ball would get kicked back by one of the blades. She counted the blades and tried to time how long it took another blade to cover the opening after the last one left.

"C'mon, lady," a teen standing behind Sawyer said. "Just hit the ball."

Sawyer whipped around. "Don't ever talk to a lady like that."

The kid opened his mouth, studied Sawyer, and backed away.

"Take all the time you want," Sawyer said, as though she were putting for the LPGA championship.

She approached her ball, wiggled her hips to get settled, watched the blades, and hit her ball. It sailed into the windmill between two turning blades. It didn't, however, drop into the hole. That was fine. She'd shown those punks who was the boss babe here.

"Great shot, Ana," Sawyer said. "I only hope I can do as well."

She didn't roll her eyes, but she wanted to. If she'd learned nothing else about Sawyer, he wasn't only competitive, but his eye-hand coordination was off the charts.

His purple ball followed hers through and dropped directly into the cup.

"Nice," the teen behind him said.

Sawyer nodded, took Ana's hand, and walked to the end of the hole, where he patiently waited as she tapped in her ball.

She grinned and pulled her ball out. "All yours," she shouted to the waiting teens.

"We're neck-and-neck," he announced after adding their strokes. "Two more holes to pull out a win."

"Hmm, are you talking to yourself for encouragement?"

He chuckled. "Maybe."

They tied the seventeenth hole, each taking a par.

"This is it, cowboy. You're going down."

He lifted an eyebrow. "Is that so?"

She heard the sexual innuendo as it left her mouth. *Really, Ana. You needed to engage brain before mouth.*

"I guess we'll see," she said, fully aware of what she was implying, but then again, did she really? She'd heard the term *to go down on a woman*, she'd read about it in books, but she had no idea what that felt like. Seemed yucky to her. Why would a guy want to put his mouth down there?

Designed to collect the golf balls at the end of the game, the eighteenth green was a simple shot into a mine shaft. There was a slight curve to the right, but shouldn't be tough. It was, in her humble opinion, the easiest hole of the course.

She set her ball down and wiggled her hips.

"That's not going to work," he whispered in her ear.

Those blasted chill bumps popped on her arms. "Umm, what isn't going to work?'

He chuckled low and deep in her ear. "You're not going to distract me by wiggling your hips. I'm on to you, lady."

She looked at him, her eyes wide with shock. "I have no idea what you mean."

"Right," he said with a laugh and stepped back to let her go first.

Her shot careened off the tee, hit the back board, and rolled back to the middle of the path.

She whirled toward him, her hands fisted on her hips. "You did that on purpose."

He put his hand on his chest. "I have no idea what you mean," he parroted back to her, then grinned. "Go on. Finish the hole."

Later, if she told this story, she would swear her poor play was due to those darned goose bumps and those were his fault, so by association, he caused her to two-putt.

He stepped up. "I hate to do this to you, hon, but…" He stroked his club. The purple ball sailed down the path and into the hole like it was metal and the hole was the world's strongest magnet.

"Not fair," she complained jokingly. "You've played this course before."

He draped his arm over her shoulders. "Ah, babe. Be the good loser I know you can be."

She laughed and bumped her hip against his. "Let's find a piano and have a real contest."

He chuckled and pulled her closer. "Yeah, I don't think so. But, I would love to hear you play." With a wink, he asked, "Can you play the theme to Star Wars?"

"Seriously? *Star Wars*? Are you a Trekkie?"

He laughed. "A Trekkie is a Star Trek fan, not Star Wars." He shook his head.

"This is so sad. Your education is obviously lacking in substance."

With a careless shrug, she said, "Whatever. They're the same thing."

He gasped. "Dear lord, woman. They aren't even close to the same thing." He pulled an imaginary notebook from his hip pocket, pretended to flip it open, and began to write.

"What are you doing?" she asked with a snort.

"Making myself a note of movies I need to rent."

She rolled her eyes.

He tucked the invisible notebook back into his pocket. "Ready for the roller coaster yet? Or maybe the zipline?"

"Go-karts."

They headed toward the racetrack, such as it was. But she couldn't stop thinking about the theme to Star Wars. He really had no idea of just how good she was, or even who she was. Man, she really liked that he wasn't buttering her up for a favor. People were always trying to get her to play for a party or a wedding —*gasp.*

The line at the go-karts was long with parents and kids.

"Let's grab a drink and wait until the line dies down," he suggested.

"Perfect."

With drinks in hand—Diet Coke for her, Mountain Dew for him—they found an empty bench and sat.

"Do you remember on the way up here that I asked your age?" he asked.

"I certainly do. Don't you know you never ask a lady her age?" She grinned so he would know she was kidding.

"I had a reason. I think, but I'm not sure, I think I've heard you play."

Her heart skittered to a stop. "What? When?"

"Back in Germany. You said you were about seven. I would have been about nine. Did you play at Schloss Kaserne in Butzbach?"

"Yes," she said hesitantly, drawing out the word.

"Did you build a snowman with a bunch of the kids who went to school on the base?"

"Maybe," she said, again hesitantly. What was going on here?

He tapped his chest. "I was one of those kids."

Her jaw sagged. "You were not."

"I was. I swear. Mom made me go to anything that

resembled culture, and you playing classical music fit the bill for her."

"Did you enjoy it?"

"Hell, no. I was nine. I wanted to hear current bands." He smiled. "But I remember the cute girl at the piano."

She dipped her head, sure her cheeks were flaming. "That was one of my earliest concerts. My piano teacher convinced my parents to let me go with a group of students who were going over to play for the troops."

"I don't remember your parents."

"Mom didn't go. She had some fund-raising event for the Chicago Philharmonic that she was in charge of and didn't want to hand it off to her co-chair. Dad went, but he spent a lot of time sampling the German beers."

"Can't blame him for that. The Germans produce excellent beer, but I don't remember meeting him, either."

"You probably didn't. In fact, I met my manager, Randall Blagg, on that trip. His son, Geoffrey, was one of the students playing."

Sawyer shook his head. "Sorry. I don't remember anyone other than some girl with long wavy hair and a big grin. You marched onto that stage with such confidence."

She laughed. "I'm sure. I thought I was hot stuff. Life got a little harder when I discovered there were a lot of talented pianists in the world. If I wanted to make it, I knew I had to up my game. Are you telling me that when you had this memory, you didn't go research my name?"

This time, his face flushed.

"Ah-ha. You did," she said with a flair.

"Yeah, okay, I looked last night."

"Why didn't you tell me?"

He grimaced. "I felt a little like a stalker. And, I confess, I was a little awed by all your awards and records."

She narrowed her eyes. "You don't seem awed."

"But I am. I'm a SEAL. I can be replaced, but someone with your talent? You only come along once in a lifetime."

"Thank you. I'm flattered."

"Bullshit. You know you're good."

She smiled shyly. "Yeah," she said, wrinkling her nose. "I know. God, I love it, too." She surprised herself with that comment. She did love it. She loved the practice, the performances, the ovations…all of it.

"So, why are you hiding in Lake Kincade and driving a beater car?"

CHAPTER 5

Sawyer waited for Ana to answer his question. After a couple of minutes of silence, he said, "Never mind. None of my business." He stood. "C'mon. Let's get in line for those race cars."

She grabbed his hand and pulled him back down. "There's a story. I promise. But..."

"But?" He arched a brow.

"I want to trust you. I mean, I do trust you, but I don't want to be found—at least, not yet."

"Okay." He dragged out the word. "I know you can afford a better car than that junker you're driving. Start there."

"First, don't insult Barbie."

"Barbie?"

"Yes, Malibu Barbie, my car. She's had a rough life."

He stifled the grin. "I can see that."

"I rescued her from a horrible used car lot."

"Well, that was good of you. How long have you had, um, Barbie?"

"She and I have been best buddies since I picked her up on Friday."

He shut his eyes with a groan. "You bought that car and took it on a road trip to Lake Kincade? Did you even look at those tires?"

She wrinkled her nose. "No. I guess I should have, but the salesman said she was in tip-top shape. After all, she'd have to be in prime condition to have gone two-hundred-and-fifty-thousand miles."

He groaned. "Oh, hon, I hope you didn't pay much for that car."

"I didn't," she said with much excitement. "I got it for only three-thousand-dollars."

Should he tell her that she probably overpaid? Nope. No reason to put a wall between Ana and Barbie.

"Well, you should probably have the engine checked if you're going to drive it much."

He wasn't sure what he'd said, but her face fell. "What's with the gloomy face?" he asked.

"Oh, nothing. I probably won't have Barbie long. I'm sure Randall or my parents will make me sell her. Besides having no place to park her, I rarely drive myself anywhere." She straightened and pointed. "Look. The line has gotten a whole lot shorter. Let's go race."

He could recognize the change in topic and went with it. But she was almost thirty. Shouldn't she be making her own decisions without Randall or her parents?

"Sounds like a good idea."

She twitched nervously as they waited their turn to drive.

"Why are you so fidgety? You've done this before,

right?" Surely, she had. Every kid growing up drove go-karts all the time.

"No. This is my first time." Her voice was excited, which matched the broad smile on her face.

"Do I need to tell you what to do?"

"I drive the car and pass you all the time, right?"

He laughed. "Exactly." Remembering her speedy driving coming into Lake Kincade, he might ease off the gas pedal just a little.

She climbed into her car, her bright smile lighting her entire face. Her eyes sparkled as she listened to the safety spiel from the teenager loading the cars. She was nodding enthusiastically with each safety instruction.

"Where's my helmet?" he heard her ask.

The teen shook his head. "Don't need no helmet on this ride. Have fun. Push the pedal to go."

She eased out of the parking area onto the track and was immediately passed by a kid of about six.

He snickered quietly and thought seriously about not driving. Watching her creep around the tiny oval track was entertainment enough. But he'd promised, so he climbed into car fifty-four and pulled out. She was coming up on his left side.

"I'm passing you," she shouted and laughed as she passed.

He stopped fighting his grin and took off after her. One of the rules was no bumping into other cars, so he got on her tail around the oval.

"I'm beating you," she yelled over her shoulder.

Sadly, his competitive streak battled with his good person persona. There shouldn't have been a battle. He should've just let her win, but he pulled alongside her.

"Race you to the finish," he challenged.

"You're on."

And darn if she didn't pull ahead of him and cut him off at the turn. Laughter bubbled up from inside him. This woman was really something. They crossed the line at the same time, Ana whooping as though they'd finished the Indy 500. Her face shone with happiness. Her eyes sparkled.

He was hooked.

"That was so much fun," she said, clinging on his arm. "What's next?"

"Upping your game, are you? Ready to try the kiddie roller coaster?" When her face lost a little of its glow, he added, "Easy ride. Kids as young as four can ride with an adult. I think, at thirty, you can do it."

"Twenty-nine."

He laughed and put his arm around her. "Sure, for four more days."

"But you'll ride with me, right?"

"We'll be snug as sardines in a can, but sure. We can ride together."

"And this is the one that you can control how fast it goes?"

He nodded. "Yelp."

"Fine. I don't want you to think I'm a big baby."

Big baby? No way.

Sexy, mature woman? *Way!*

With his arm still draped around her shoulders, they walked over to the Runaway Rail Car roller coaster. Ana didn't have a confident expression. Her eyes were shifting nervously from side to side as she watched other riders load into the cars. Then a woman and a child of about six climbed in to ride. Sawyer noticed that the child and Ana both wore identical expressions of concern. The car rolled out of the station and hit the first curve. The child laughed and squealed with delight. That might have been when Ana decided to ride. Or maybe his powers of persuasion had convinced her. Or maybe she felt protected by him. Whatever the decision-making impetus was, he didn't care.

Ana looked at him, smiled, and said, "Okay, frog-man. My life is in your hands."

He one-arm hugged her. "I gotcha, babe."

After climbing the stairs to wait to load into a car, Ana stood in front of him, her back pressed to his chest. He would've sworn he could hear her heart racing, but he'd done this ride more than once. It wasn't scary, and he could control the speed to make her more comfortable.

"You'll be fine," he whispered in her ear.

She whimpered. It was a low, sexy sound that vibrated against his chest. It was at that moment he wondered what she would sound like during sex. Would she moan? Would she whimper when he got his face between her luscious thighs and tasted what he knew would be the sweetest nectar? Would she cry out when she came? Would she call his name with her climax?

"Next," the teen running the ride said. "You two. Are you gonna ride or just block the line?"

Sawyer straightened his back and glared at the kid. "We're riding," he growled.

Ana did that sexy moan again, but climbed into the front of the car. Sawyer slipped in behind her.

"I gotcha," he said in a low voice. "Hold on to those grab bars at your side. Just tell me what you want me to do."

He hoped he'd get to say that last sentence in a different setting and for a totally different reason.

The teen was giving him instructions on how to operate the car as Sawyer and Ann fastened their seatbelts. "Push the lever for faster, pull for slower. I think you can do it, big guy."

Sawyer had to internally laugh at the wiseass kid. Someday, that kid would be him, and some snotnosed teen would sneer at him like he was grandpa out for the day from the nursing home. He chuckled as the car began to move.

He and Ana were smashed together in the small car. The only way they could get any closer would be to remove their clothes. He doubted a piece of dental floss could slide between them.

Not that he was complaining, because he wasn't. This was like having her in his arms. He liked it… maybe more than he should.

They came to the first turn, and he pulled back on the handle to slow the car. Coming out of the curve, he said, "See? That wasn't so bad, right?"

She nodded. "Can we try a little faster?"

"Sure." He could go fast. He could go slow. He could let her be in charge even when he was on top.

Pushing the lever forward, the car sped up. In the back of his mind, he thought he'd read somewhere the maximum speed the car could obtain was twenty-five mph. Child's play. Then, he thought again about her speed, or lack thereof, on the highway. Maybe he'd push it a tad and see how she responded. After all, he believed she had way more courage and strengths than she thought she did. Walking on a stage to play the piano with a full orchestra backup? That sounded terrifying to him.

The car sped up. Ana squealed and laughed.

"Faster," she said as they rounded a curve.

Ahead was the highest climb and fall of the ride, except for one near the end. The track clicked and clacked as their small car was pulled up, and up, and up.

"Oh…my…gosh. Sawyer."

"Hang on." He meant hang onto the grab bars on the side of the car, but she instead wrapped her arms around his legs that bracketed her. He wasn't complaining.

They hit the top, which rolled along flat for about five seconds, and then rolled downhill into a large cloverleaf loop. Ana screamed. Maybe he should have slowed? Then, he heard her laughing maniacally.

"Faster," she called. "Make it go faster."

He laughed. "Babe, this is about as fast as it will go."

"No brakes," she shouted.

He grinned and pushed the lever as far forward as it would go. As they rolled along the track, they passed over the go-kart area and under the chairlift. A couple of times, the track ran over and under itself with other riders' cars passing above and below. Throughout the ride, Ana laughed and shrieked. He could only interpret those sounds as she was enjoying herself.

As they neared the end, the car slowed.

"No," she said over her shoulder. "Faster."

He chuckled. "Look who's the speed demon now. And I'm not slowing the car. We're rolling back into the station, and the conveyor belt is controlling our sped."

"Boo," she said. "This ride is too short."

He shook his head with a grin.

She climbed out of the car brimming with energy. "Let's do it again."

"Let's eat lunch and then talk about it."

She wrapped her arms around his bicep. "That was so much fun."

"I thought you might enjoy it. Are you hungry?"

"I shouldn't be, but yeah. I could eat a burger or something."

He thought about how much she'd enjoyed cooking hot dogs and s'mores last night, after confessing Randall never allowed her to eat what he called "junk food." Well, for as long as he had her, Sawyer would give her whatever her heart desired.

They found an empty picnic table, which Ana grabbed and held while he went to get them lunch. Standing in line, Sawyer glanced over his shoulder at Ana. Sitting in the bright sun, the highlights in her hair glimmered. The smile she sent him almost brought him to his knees. This woman was something special, and he doubted she knew it.

He set two double cheeseburgers on the table, along with a large order of fries, and two soft drinks. "I didn't know what you wanted on the burger, so I had them put on everything. That way, you can take off whatever you don't want. Didn't know if you wanted fries, so I got a big order so we can share."

"Works for me." She peeled back the paper on the burger, removed the top bun, and studied the lettuce, tomatoes, pickles, and onions. "As much as I really want that onion, I won't do that to you." She lifted the onion off. "You can thank me later."

"So, tell me more about your work, Ana."

She arched an eyebrow. "I could ask you the same question."

"True." He took a big bite, chewed, and then said, "But I asked first. What's a typical day like?"

She swallowed the burger bite in her mouth, and then sipped her drink. "Typical day. Hmm. I guess that depends on the day. If I have an upcoming concert, I'll get up about eight and be at the piano by nine. If I'm learning a new piece, it's a long, boring day of hearing me play the same piece over and over and over. If it's a piece I know, I'll play it a few times. Other days, if I'm playing with an orchestra, I'll work with their director on which musical pieces we'll be performing and the order." She shrugged as she dragged a French fry through a glob of ketchup. "The next day is more of the same."

He frowned. "What about fun? What do you for fun? Dates? Meeting friends for drinks?"

"There are only so many hours in a day. If I want to be the best, then something had to go."

She gave him that shrug that suggested she didn't care, but he wasn't sure he bought it.

"So, you don't date? Go to movies? Play?"

"I date…some."

His heart skipped. "You have a boyfriend?"

She wrinkled her nose. "Not really," she said with a long sigh.

"What does that mean? Either you have a special guy or you don't." His brow furrowed.

She took a big bite of her burger. He was positive that was her way of not answering or some stalling practice. But dammit, he wanted to know the truth. If she was hiding, as he suspected she was, what or who was she hiding from and why?

"You know, Ana, I'm a good listener. I won't pass judgement on anything you tell me."

Her shoulders sagged. "I know." She sighed. "I'm supposed to be in San Diego for a three-night performance, and that was after three nights in New York, and four nights in Orlando. I can't remember the last time I've had more than two consecutive days off. I've woken up and not had a clue where I was—what city I mean.

"One of the challenges is each orchestra director has a different idea about the music to be performed and in what order. San Diego was no different. I'd been in San Diego practicing for a week but…I don't know. My timing felt odd. I felt off."

She picked up her Diet Coke and pulled a long drink through the straw.

He waited, sure there was more to the story.

"Thursday, after practice, one of the girls who worked in ticket sales stumbled on me sitting on the back row after everyone left. She sat down and listened to me whine." She shook her head. "I know, I know. I have so much, but there I was crying and complaining. I should've been embarrassed, but I swear, I was numb and scared. I wasn't *me*, you know? The girl, Grace, sat and listened. I told her about Randall, and his son, and my parents. Everything poured out of me. Finally, she said, 'Screw 'em. Take a vacation.'

She shook her head with a sad smile. "I laughed and said 'Randall would kill me,'" and she said, 'Not if he can't find you.' It sounded crazy. Run away?" She chuckled and then sighed. "I guess everyone harbors runaway fantasies, right? You run and leave all your problems behind."

Sawyer let out a long breath and said quietly, "You know that doesn't work, right?"

"But isn't that kind of what you do?"

He sat back. "What?"

"You don't join any specific SEAL team. You jump from team to team; I assume leaving problems behind. You live in a motorhome that you move from location to location, again leaving problems behind."

He was stunned. Was that what he did? His entire life he'd moved, sometimes leaving bad schools, or bullies behind. He rarely left behind friends since he wasn't anywhere long enough to make many, except for those years in Germany.

"We aren't talking about me," he said, deflecting the need to think about himself. "How did you end up with Barbie?"

"Ah, Barbie," she said, nodding. "Once I decided to take an unplanned vacation, I said something about renting a car. Grace reminded me that most rentals have a tracking device in case someone runs off with a car. If I rented, and Randall or my parents were determined to find me, the rental company could probably locate the car. She suggested I buy a car. Grace's second cousin owns the car lot. She drove me down and I bought the car. She's the one who told me about Harbin's Harbor Cabins."

"But registration? Payment? And can't Grace just confess where you are?"

This time, she grinned. "It'll take forever for California to issue any type of car title. I wrote a check on a Chicago bank, so that might take a while to clear. And Grace doesn't work in ticket sales any longer. She bought a bar-slash-small restaurant in Coronado, so she won't be around. It'll take longer than a week to find her. In the meantime, I get a break." She propped her head in her hand. "It was this, or have a total meltdown. I dread facing the music when I get back." She grinned. "Pun intended."

Sawyer studied her for a moment with his lips pursed. "Then the plan for the week should be help Ana have fun and relax…?"

"Exactly."

"With me?"

Her grin widened. "Yes, with you. I thought I'd sit around read a book, but doing all these things I never get to do, or haven't ever done…well, that's what I want to do, now."

He returned her smile. "Then, that's the plan. Any suggestions for what you want to do?"

"I definitely want to go out on the lake. I've never fished."

He pulled the imaginary notepad from his pocket again and made an imaginary note, which made her laugh. "Got it. What else?"

"Live music—that I'm not providing. I saw in the list of activities that there's a band playing at the town amphitheater, wherever that is."

"I saw that. I know where it is. Parking is tight, so that means taking my bike."

"I'm okay with that, as long as you're okay with helmet hair."

He laughed. "I can manage. I don't remember much about the band. Do you?"

"Country music, I think." She shrugged. "As long as it's not Bach or Mozart, I'll be fine." She grinned. "I can be a tough judge. You wouldn't have a good time."

"I get it. I watch military shows or movies and want to throw my boot at the screen while yelling, 'It doesn't work like that.'"

"I bet."

"Ready to head back, or do you want to do the roller coaster again?"

She grinned. "One more time on the coaster, please."

Like the first time, she laughed at every turn and every dip. This time, however, he barely used the brake, taking them full speed, or as much as the ride allowed, which produced howls of laughter and delighted screams. His heart and memory savored every laugh, every thrilled scream.

She climbed from the stopped car and wrapped her arm around his waist. "I'm so dizzy, I'm going to hold on to you for a minute."

His heart raced up his throat and lodged there, making swallowing and breathing difficult. Hell, yeah, she could hold on to him.

He slung his arm over her shoulders. "I've got you."

She chuckled. "I feel like my head is spinning. So, now I know."

"Know what?" he asked with a frown.

"Only one roller coaster ride per visit."

"Well, we have two ways to get down the mountain to the car. One, we can take the same chair lift down that we rode up. Or we can do the bobsled ride. It starts here and ends in the parking lot." He felt her shoulders tense under his arm. "The bobsled sounds a lot worse than the ride is. It's fun. I promise."

"All things considered, I think I'd like to take the chair lift back down. This time I'll be able to keep my eyes open and see everything."

"Okay. I love the lift. Leaving now will give us time to get home and chill for a while. There are fireworks over the lake tonight. I'm not sure what time, but we could do dinner and go back to the cabin to see the fireworks or use the firepit again. Maybe catch some fish from the bank and fry them up for dinner."

"That sounds like fun, but I think I'll take a short nap this afternoon."

"Or maybe read?"

"Or read."

"Something that's going to make you throw a book at me again?"

She laughed. "Sexy romance. I think I'll stay in that lane."

He liked that idea...a lot.

She loaded onto the chairlift like a pro. Bent her knees and was ready to be scooped up. Once they were settled and moving, Sawyer held out his hand palm up. She glanced at him, smiled, and laced her fingers through his.

Her fingers were thin but muscular. Her nails were polished with a shiny light pink. Holding her hand made his heart race. He liked Ana. He would be sorry to see their time end. Would she?

CHAPTER 6

Back at Harbin's, they went their separate ways… her to take a nap, and him? She had no idea. She was enjoying their time together. Sometimes, she found it hard to believe they'd only known each other for two days, well, if she didn't consider their meeting as children. She'd laughed more in the past forty-eight hours than she had in years. The weight on her shoulders had lessened, but the muscles were still tight and achy. A massage sounded like a message from heaven. Too bad today was Sunday and tomorrow was a holiday. Maybe later in the week?

When she finally awoke, the sun was low on the horizon. Automatically, she reached for her phone to check messages, and then stopped. Her phone was off and had been since early Friday morning. She was sure she had messages, verbal and text, from Randall, Geoffrey, and her mother. She suspected her email box had taken a few hits from those three as well. As much as she was curious about what they'd actually said, she wasn't crazy enough to start her phone.

She showered and dressed in jeans, sneakers, and a long-sleeve shirt. During the day, the sun kept the temperatures pleasantly warm, but if they were going to sit outside to watch fireworks, she'd need clothes that covered her arms and legs. She's felt a pang of guilt as she'd told Sawyer they could fish this afternoon after her nap, but the nap had lasted much longer than she'd planned. She'd needed sleep and rest, something no one around her seemed to understand.

After pouring the last of the merlot into a glass, she stepped onto her porch to watch the lake activity, which, in her opinion, was more entertaining than any television show. The firepit had been cleaned out and fresh wood stood ready to light. For the next half-hour, she sat and enjoyed the quiet swish of the breeze through the trees, the occasional chirp of birds, the roar of boats as they sped along the lake, but mostly, she enjoyed the peace in her soul. Is this how the rest of the world felt? She'd been on her hamster wheel for so long, she'd forgotten what it was like having nothing pressing to do.

She heard his whistle before she saw Sawyer. He was walking along the sandy shore of the lake. A fishing pole dangled over one shoulder while he carried a small plastic box in the other hand. She was glad to see he'd gone on without her. As nice as he was being, she didn't want to do anything that would mess up his vacation.

"Hey, sleepyhead," he said with a smile. "Have a nice nap?"

"I did. Where's all the fish?" she joked.

"Still in the lake," he said. "But I promised each one that we'd be back."

"Sounds like a plan, or maybe it's a threat?"

He laughed.

She gestured toward him with her wine glass. "Where'd you get all the fishing stuff?"

He pointed toward the office with the plastic box. "Mandy. She has fishing equipment for guests. I'm headed up there to return it. Want to walk along?"

"I need some exercise, so sure," she replied as she stood and bounded off the porch. "Have fun?"

"I did." He glanced over at her. "But it would've been more fun with your company."

Heat flushed her cheeks. "Sorry. I think it's all the fresh air. I just crashed when we got back."

He nudged her with his shoulder. "I'm glad you got some rest. From the description of your usual days, sounds like you need fresh air and sleep. Oh, remind me to ask Mandy about the fireworks tonight—where the best place to see them is and what time."

"Will do."

Activity teemed in the parking lot, families coming and going into and out of cabins. Children with wet bathing suits and hair dripping with lake water climbed wearily from cars and headed into different cabins. Drained parents pulled damp towels and beach bags from the trunks of cars and followed their exhausted offspring inside. From one cabin, a baby cried. From another, a pair of children argued over the television until an adult voice put the verbal brawl to an end.

Ana had never spent much time around other children. Her piano lessons had started at such as early age and had taken so much of her time that attending a typical school had never fit the schedule. She'd had tutors and home teachers most of her life, until college. It was only there that she'd had to share her education with others, and those individuals had been adults.

"Did you miss having brothers and sisters?" she asked.

He shrugged. "I don't know." He glanced over. "My birthday is near Christmas. People used to ask me if I'd rather have had a birthday in the summer or some time other than December. I couldn't answer because I'd never known anything else, know what I mean? Did you?"

She shook her head. "I don't think so. My parents had busy lives, so maybe it would've been cool to have had a sister to play with, but I read so many stories about how siblings never get along, or how parents play favorites that I ended up deciding when I was about ten that things in my house were fine. Having another child would've been too much work for my parents. I mean, I know they loved me, but they were so busy with, well, everything else." She smiled at him. "How close to Christmas is your birthday?"

"The eighteenth. Far enough away to avoid the dreaded birthday-slash-Christmas present duo. My folks were good about making sure my birthday was a completely different holiday from Christmas. I didn't appreciate their effort as much as a child as I do now."

They reached the office. He opened the door and allowed her to enter first.

"Good afternoon. How was the fishing, Sawyer?" Mandy's voice was chipper and happy. "Where's all the fish?"

He quirked the corner of his mouth. "Fishing was good, but I did catch and release so Ana and I can catch them again later this week." He walked over to the stand that held fishing rods and reels and returned his to its spot. "But it was a nice day to be out."

Mandy looked at Ana. "You didn't want to fish with Sawyer?"

Ana grinned. "I opted for the long afternoon nap."

Mandy sighed. "Sounds like heaven."

"It was. Thank you for leaving my key on the door the other night. I meant to get up here and tell you."

"No problem," Mandy replied with a shrug. "Happy to do it."

"Mandy," Sawyer said. "I was telling Ana about the fireworks Lake Kincade does for Labor Day. Do you know when they go off?"

"Tonight, about nine or nine-fifteen. Depends on the weather. Organizers wait until it gets dark, so that's my guess."

"And the best spot to watch them?"

Mandy chuckled. "At the water's edge in front of your cabin."

Ana looked at Sawyer. "Perfect, right?"

"Right."

"Haven't seen you jogging by the office this year, Sawyer. You're still in the SEALs, right?"

He nodded. "You will tomorrow." He patted his stomach. "I've eaten too much good food on this trip. I have to burn some of the calories." He looked at Ana. "Want to come with me in the morning?"

"Jogging?" Ana laughed. "I doubt I could run a mile, but don't let me stop you."

"Wear a shirt this time," Mandy said. "Last year, you almost caused two car accidents from female drivers ogling you."

He scoffed. "That did not happen."

Mandy held up her hand as through swearing a

vow. "It did." She looked Ana. "He's a menace on the roads."

Ana laughed.

"And we're leaving," Sawyer said. "Oh, we'll need to rent a boat for…." He looked at Ana with a raised eyebrow. "Wednesday?"

She nodded.

"Wednesday," he said with finality to Mandy. "Can you reserve one for us?"

"Pontoon or bass boat?"

"Pontoon, I think." Sawyer glanced at Ana, who nodded her agreement.

Mandy made a notation on the desk calendar. "Got you covered." She looked up. "Good thing you didn't want one for tomorrow. We are completely booked." With a shrug, she added, "Labor Day, you know?"

"I wouldn't want to be out there tomorrow. The water will be choppy as hell."

"True. Okay, then, I've got your reservation for Wednesday. Anything else?"

"Not for me. Ana?"

Ana shook her head. "Can't think of a thing."

Sawyer snapped his fingers. "Dinner. It's getting late. Any suggestions for where we can grab a meal?"

"DD's is always good. There's Hardwick Bar-B-Que or maybe Elaine's, if you're in the mood for steak."

On the walk back their cabins, Sawyer took Ana's hand. "Dinner. What do you think about trying Elaine's for steak?"

"Works for me."

Dinner was as good as Mandy had promised. Actually, it was better. Their filets were buttery soft and grilled to perfection.

As they pulled Ana's car back into the parking area

of Harbin's Harbor Cabins, they were shocked to see a chain across the drive. When they stopped, a teenage boy hurried from the office and over to the driver's window.

"Parking for cabins only, please," he said.

"We're staying here," Sawyer said. "Cabins ten and twelve. Beckett and Cristiano."

The teen checked his clipboard and nodded. "Sorry for the inconvenience. With the fireworks, too many people try to park here and take up all our residents' spaces." He unlocked the chain, and it fell to the ground. Sawyer drove over it and into the lot.

"Thanks," Sawyer said.

"Have a nice time," the teen called and pulled the chain back across the drive.

"Well, I guess viewing is good here if Mandy has to protect the lot."

"Sounds like it." He parked in the spot for cabin ten. "I didn't take our chairs down to the water before we left. I was worried they'd be occupied when we got back."

"Good thought."

"I'll do that now before I fix a drink to carry down."

"I'm changing into shorts. I'll meet you at the water."

Ana hurried into her cabin to change. Her stomach was pleasantly full. Her mood was better than it'd been in months. Grace had been right with her, "Screw 'em. Take a vacation," advice. She wasn't getting as much rest as she'd thought she would. However, she wasn't complaining. Sawyer had turned out to be a sexy, enjoyable way to spend some time.

After slipping into shorts and a T-shirt that boasted "I'm All Fingers," she poured a glass of merlot from a new bottle, slipped on her sneakers, and headed down to the lake. Sawyer was already there and sitting in one of the chairs when she walked up.

"That's not a beer," she said as she took the chair beside him.

"Bourbon. Beer with hot dogs works, but most of the time, I'd rather be sipping a nice Kentucky bourbon."

"Can I taste?"

He handed her the glass.

She took a sip. Fire burned all the way down her throat until the liquid splashed into her stomach. Her eyes watered. "Not at all what I expected."

He took back his glass with a smile. "Life never is," he said, with a lift of his glass.

She slipped off her sneakers and dug her toes into the sand. Water lapping at her toes tickled. As she took a sip of her wine, she sagged against the back of the chair. "Ahh," she said with a sigh. "This feels wonderful."

"It does, don't it?" he replied. "Think it's the setting or the company?"

A smile bloomed on her mouth. "Why can't it be both?"

"It can, I suppose. For me, it's the company."

Her smile widened. "Thank you. When I was changing clothes, I was thinking about how great these days have been."

"And we have a few more before we're required to go back to reality."

"Oh, let's not go back. We can run away to some tropical island and sit on the beach all day."

He chuckled. "I'm in, but I'll need you to explain to the Navy why I went AWOL."

She snapped her fingers. "No problem."

"Right," he said with a snort. "The military is known for being all caring and considerate about deserters."

With a sigh, she said, "I hear you saying I'd be visiting you in some horrible military jail, right?"

"You'd come to visit?" He put his hand over his heart. "I'm touched."

She chuckled. "Of course, I'd visit. Any time I was in the states, I'd make it a point to visit."

"I'm thinking you wouldn't get to come often what with your international tour schedule." He looked at her. "I checked your schedule today. I'm glad we have this week. From the looks of your upcoming appearances, you'll be overseas some in the coming weeks."

"I know." She blew out a long breath. "But we still have a few days. Let's make the most of them."

"I hate to be a killjoy, but your family and your manager must be worried about you."

She shrugged. "I'm sure if I turned on my phone, it'd be filled with text and voice messages, but if I don't know, I can't respond, right?" She looked at him. "I don't want to talk about that anymore tonight."

He nodded.

From behind them, they heard a couple of voices coming closer. Ana glanced over her shoulder toward the sound. "It's Mandy and a man coming this way."

"Hey, fellow fireworks watchers," Mandy called out. "Can we join you? You're hogging the best spot."

Sawyer stood. "Of course. Let me help you." He took the collapsible chair Mandy carried and placed it in the sand next to Ana. "Sawyer Beckett," he said to the man and extended his hand.

"Aaron Harbin, Mandy's husband."

"Nice to meet you."

Ana leaned over with a wave. "I'm Ana."

Aaron acknowledged her greeting with a smile and return wave.

"Have any trouble getting back into the lot?" Mandy asked.

"No. The teen manning the chain was very polite."

Mandy looked at Aaron and both of them chuckled.

"That's our son, Douglas. I think he likes all the power he perceives goes with that job."

Ana chuckled. "Well, he did a good job."

"That's a relief," Aaron said around his wife.

At that moment, a large boom echoed across the water and the sky lit up with bright multi-colored sparkles.

Sawyer held out his hand, and Ana took it. Then, she settled into her chair to watch the fireworks in the sky, which didn't come close to the fireworks taking place inside her. Sawyer had said that life can hold surprises. Well, life had certainly thrown her a curveball with him. She was thankful they'd found each other, but sad knowing their time was limited to this week.

But was it? Limited to this week? Who said so?

One thing she was positive of…Sawyer made her feel things she'd never felt around another man, especially Geoffrey Blagg. To think that she'd given thought to actually marrying him. Not a lot of *serious* thought, but consideration nonetheless. And why? Because her mother and Randall, Geoffrey's father, had both felt that Geoffrey would be supportive of her career, and even ready to step into the managerial role as soon as Randall retired, not that he had any plans to do so.

Her mother had even gone so far as to suggest that Ana should take Geoffrey as a husband since he'd probably be the only contender. Her own mother thought her incapable of drawing the attention of another man. She'd told Ana on many occasions that men would be after her money more than her personality.

The thought infuriated her while at the same time making her extremely sad. Her current reality was that no men had asked her for dates nor expressed any interest in her...until Sawyer. Now that she'd felt the attraction and attention from a man like Sawyer, how could she go back to her lonely life?

Good question. All she knew for sure was Geoffrey Blagg was not the answer.

CHAPTER 7

S ince they had tickets for the Labor Day concert, Sawyer and Ana opted to hang around their cabins all day. Well, that was partially true. Ana sat on her front porch, and so did Sawyer. Sure, he could have sat on his own porch, but where was the fun in that?

"You enjoy the fireworks last night?"

Ana slipped a piece of paper between two pages of the book in her hand. "I did. What is it about fireworks that brings out the kid in all of us?"

He snorted. "I don't know, but they do. What's the coolest place you've ever watched fireworks?"

She set her book on the arm of her chair. "Tough question. Let me think. Hmm, watching fireworks in London was pretty cool. I was in Sydney, Australia for New Year's Eve one year. Those were massive. There's something special about each time that makes it stand out from the rest." She gave him a shy smile. "Last night, holding your hand for the show will make it one I don't forget."

His heart melted at her words. The firmly constructed wall around his emotions dropped a brick or two. He held out his hand, which she took. After lacing their fingers together, he said, "Me, too," and squeezed her fingers. Three days into meeting a woman who made his pulse quicken and his breathing labored, and he hadn't even kissed her yet. Crazy, but he understood why.

Ana was special.

Kissing her would be special.

Loving her would be more than special. He feared it would be transcendental, and that unnerved him. How did one go back to ordinary after an experience like that?

He sighed. "I've got to get moving."

With a frown, she asked. "To where?"

"I promised myself I'd get in a ten-mile run today, and it's already noon." He lifted their joint hands and kissed her knuckles. "Want to run along with me?"

She laughed. Not a chuckle. Not a scoff. A full-blown laugh that came from her gut. "No," she gasped out. "Not only no, but heck, no."

He grinned. "Heck, no? Whew. That's some strong language from you."

Again, she laughed. "Heck, yeah, on the language. Heck, no, on the run. But you have fun." She swept her free hand around the porch. "I'll be right here when you get back."

"I'll probably be gone a couple of hours. Want me to bring some food back when I come?"

She looked at him, her smile so bright it shamed the sun. "Seriously? You'd stop for food for me and jog back carrying it?" She shook her head. "Let me get dinner for us. When you get back, how about a pizza?"

He stood. "And that's why I have to run today." He leaned over to kiss her and paused. Leaning over to give her a quick kiss felt natural, like something he did every day. To his relief, she arched her face toward him and their lips met. Her lips were soft, and he'd expected that. But he hadn't prepared himself for her taste, nor the sucker punch to his gut that his simple kiss produced.

When he stepped back, he looked into a pair of sparkling green eyes that accompanied Ana's smile. "Well, that took you long enough," she said.

He grinned, and kissed her a second time. "I see I'll have to make up for lost time."

She chuckled. "See that you do."

Pulling himself away from her was tough, like super-magnet connection tough, but after a third kiss, he straightened, shook his head, and walked down the stairs. "I'll be back in a couple of hours."

"I'll be waiting."

He took one last look, smiled, and turned away. This might be the fastest run in his life. Jogging through the parking area, he waved at Mandy through the office window and hit the main drag. He'd clocked the mileage on a previous trip, so he knew how far he had to run out of town to reach five miles before turning back. Something told him today's run would feel like twenty instead of ten.

At the five-mile mark, he jogged across the road and began his trek back to Harbin's. He lifted his T-shirt to wipe his face, and four cars hooted horns. Lowering the wet material, he grinned. Four cars of women had pulled to the shoulder of the road across from him and were waving out the windows. With a chuckle, he returned their waves and jogged on, not in the least tempted to collect a name or number from any of them.

As he passed DD's Diner, a group of teenage girls stood huddled outside the door. One of them yelled, "Hey, baby," at him. A giggling titter ran through the group. If only he'd had that kind of response from girls that age when he was that age. Now, it was an invitation to visit the local jail. Still, he smiled, waved, and hurried on.

He checked his time, not surprised to find he was on pace to beat his own record. He turned into Harbin's lot, jogged to where his and Ana's cabins were located, and headed straight for the lake. His pace barely slowed as he hit the water and waded in until he could submerge his entire body.

The water was cold; his body was hot. He was sure steam was pouring off him as he waded back up the bank. His leather trainers were accustomed to the abuse, but then again, he knew how to take care of the leather. His shirt was plastered to his chest and back. His shorts clung to his thighs but that didn't deter the rough water from trying to pull them down his hips.

Slinging the water out of his hair and off his face, he looked up to find Ana standing on her porch, leaning on the railing. The expression on her face was one of pure lust. The corner of his mouth quirked up.

"Hey, babe. Wanna take a swim?" he called. "Water's rough and cold, but I'll protect you."

A grin stretched across her mouth. "If you weren't wearing that shirt, you'd look like Poseidon rising from the sea."

"You mean like this?" He stripped his shirt over his head and held his arms out to the side.

She licked her lips. "Um, yeah. Darn it for not having a camera."

He laughed and walked onto her porch. "C'mon here," he said, his arm outstretched and dripping water. "Give me a kiss."

She screamed with laughter and raced for her door. "Don't get me wet. Sawyer! Don't…"

He grabbed her from behind, wrapping her in his arms. "Hmm. You smell good," he said, nuzzling her neck with his nose.

Still laughing, she turned and wrapped her arms around his neck. "Might as well get both sides wet, I guess."

Her T-shirt covered breasts pressed against him, soaking up the water from his damp chest; the places they touched warmed from her body heat. His stomach flipped. His breath caught in surprise at her actions. A smile stretched his mouth. "I like how you think, Ms. Cristiano." He leaned down to kiss her, insanely pleased when she met him halfway.

"Your lips are cold," she said with a grin. "And you taste like…" She flicked out her tongue and touched his bottom lip. "Lake water."

He arched a brow. "Is that a problem?"

"Not for me"

"Thank God." He put a hand at the back of her head and held her against him as his mouth took hers in a clash of lips and tongues. Where he was sure and confident in his actions, hers seemed hesitant, almost tentative, as though trying out something new and different.

When he angled his head to take the kiss deeper, she followed his lead. When he licked her lips, she opened, and he thrust his tongue inside. She gasped and clung to him, her tongue touching his with short, almost timid strokes. Thanks to Joey at music camp, he knew she wasn't technically a virgin, but he began to question exactly how little experience she had. If it was as little as he was beginning to suspect, her turning in his arms and licking his lip was a huge risk on her part. A quiet moan vibrated in her throat. His cock surged to full erection.

Someone cleared his throat.

With a groan, Sawyer reluctantly pulled his mouth away from Ana's. Her eyes stared at him, glazed with wonderment and lust.

"Um, sorry, man. Pizza for Ana."

Sawyer turned toward the teen standing beside the porch, a large square pizza box in his hands. "Thanks. What do we owe you?"

Ana stepped back. "I've got this." She pulled a couple of twenties from her front pocket—damp from being pressed against his wet shorts. "Sorry," she said to the delivery teen. She tilted her head toward Sawyer. "He got me wet." Her eyes popped open as though hearing the implications of her words. She thrust the bills out. "Keep the change."

The teen smirked. "Thanks." He looked at Sawyer with a cocky grin. "Keep up the good work, man." He whipped around and hurried off.

Sawyer shook his head with a chuckle. "I think we scared off the pizza guy."

"Doubtful. I gave him a big tip. I suspect he'll volunteer to come back anytime."

With a glance down at his naked chest and wet shorts, he said, "I'm going to run to my cabin and take the quickest shower of my life." He paused, then gave her the smile that had never failed to get him a date.

"Unless you want to join me? We do have microwaves."

Her face flushed. "Join you? In the shower?" The last question was asked with a choked voice that cracked.

He would bet his entire monthly paycheck she's never showered with a guy, if the shocked look on her face was any indication.

"Maybe next time," he said and winked. "Be right back."

He flipped his wet shirt over his shoulder and raced to his cabin, stopping only long enough to glance back at cabin ten. Ana's fingers were pressed to her lips. He watched as her knees buckled and she dropped into a chair. A self-satisfied grin grew on his mouth. He'd done that, and if he had his way, those wouldn't be the last kisses of their day, nor their week.

After stripping off his remaining wet clothes and shoes, he hung the clothes to dry and set the trainers by the rotating fan in his living room. Navy showers were infamous for the brevity, but his shower that day might have set a speed record. The only element that had slowed him down was his hair. He needed a trim, or maybe closer to a cut. Women seemed to love his long hair, and he loved that fact. However, the time it took to wash and condition it was time wasted when he could be with Ana. Their time together was limited, and he didn't want to squander a second of it.

His back was still a little damp when he pulled on a T-shirt, jumped into a pair of shorts, and jammed his feet into sandals. Since he wasn't completely dry, he opted for commando, but that would be his secret. His sweet date might faint if she were aware. After grabbing a couple of beers—because what went better with pizza than beer?—he raced back to Ana's cabin, where he found her sitting on the front porch. The small porch table, which had been over to the side now stood between the chairs, napkins, forks, and plates set out for lunch. Internally, he smiled. Who used forks for pizza? Probably sweet, sweet Ana did.

"Smells wonderful," he said, noticing that she had also changed clothes. "I forgot to ask what kind of pizza you ordered." He crossed his fingers it wasn't vegetarian. He liked vegetables as much as the next man, but pizza without meat was insane.

She gave him a withering, eye-rolling expression. "Seriously? All meat. I told them to put every meat they had on it."

He chuckled and opened the box lid. "Let's see. Sausage. Canadian bacon. Crumbled bacon. Ham. Pepperoni. And is that prosciutto?"

"And extra cheese. All that meat needed some cheese."

"I think I'm in love."

She laughed. "Well, I appreciate your love for the pizza, but you have to share."

Except he wasn't talking about the pizza.

"Brought beers," he said, holding up the six-pack of green glass bottles.

"I have Diet Cokes," she replied, lifting her plastic bottle.

"Then I think we're ready."

He tilted his bottle toward her and she tapped it with her soft drink. Then he lifted a piece of pizza, pinched the sides together, and took a big bite. As he chewed, he looked at her astonished face. "What?"

She held up a fork in an unspoken question.

He laughed. "Darlin', nobody uses forks for pizza."

"Oh, okay." She lifted the smallest piece, folded it like he had, and took a bite. She groaned as she chewed. Damn, he loved her groans, but he'd especially would love to hear one in a bed.

"This is so good," she said, covering her mouth with her hand. "I almost never get to have pizza."

"That sounds criminal."

She laughed. "I never eat like we have this week. I've got to get back on my regular diet or none of my performance gowns are going to fit."

"Which one is your favorite?"

"I have this burgundy one that looks great."

He sat back with his pizza and beer and let her talk. It was one of the first times she'd really opened up about her life on the road. It didn't sound horrible, but it did sound exhausting, and this from a guy who could function for days with fifteen-minute naps. He envied her talent, but that was about all he envied.

As she described her life and her days, he realized how similar their lives were. Both of them practiced their jobs daily until performance was muscle memory more than mental memory. Both of them had careers that required travel, even if his travel was more covert than hers. They each had a person driving their careers...A manager for her and the Navy for him. Given the things she'd said about her manager, he might have the better deal with the Navy.

Nonetheless, he enjoyed listening to her talk. He loved her voice and how her strongest cussword was heck. He loved how her hair shone in the afternoon sun as it dropped toward the lake.

As they talked, he consumed the vast majority of the pizza; however, Ana did eat three pieces, which he suspected was huge for her.

"Great pizza," he said, patting his belly. "How did you know which pizza place to order from?"

"Oh, I walked up to the office and asked Mandy. She told me she'd seen you run by. She also said she was glad you were wearing a shirt."

He laughed.

"Did you make it the full ten miles?" she asked.

"I did. Probably closer to twelve by the time I headed back."

"And how many women tried to pick you up?"

He wasn't a man who embarrassed easily. If he had been, he would never have survived childhood. And, if Mandy hadn't made a point about his shirt, and women watching him run, he probably wouldn't have given any thought to the four cars of women who had honked and waved, nor the teenage girls who had giggled and shouted at him. But he'd noticed, and now, he felt a heat in his cheeks, which made Ana gasp and then howl with laughter.

"Ohmygod," she said between gales of laughter. "I was kidding, but some woman tried to pick you up?"

He gave a self-depreciating shrug. "There were a few."

"A few?" Her mouth gaped. "How many is a few?"

"I don't know because I only have eyes for you."

She smiled. "That was a very good answer, Sawyer."

A good answer and a real answer, he thought. Who wanted the apples off the ground when he held the choicest one in his hand?

"We probably want to get ready for the show tonight," he said as a way to change the subject.

Her hand reached out and then she groaned. "What time is it? I'm so used to checking the time on my phone."

He checked the watch he always wore. "Close to six."

"You're kidding," she said with a gasp. "I can't believe we've been sitting here talking for four hours."

"Time passes fast with good company."

She smiled. "Thank you."

"Put on some long pants," he suggested. "We probably want to head out soon. Parking will be tight."

She grinned. "Not with your bike. I bet we have no problem at all."

Once the unused plates and forks were returned to her kitchen, Sawyer left to put on jeans and grab a jacket. He doubted it would be needed, but the night could get cool before they returned, and he hated the idea that Ana could get cold.

She was waiting for him on her porch and hurried down to meet him as soon as he stepped off his porch.

"I'm excited." Her face was lit with her smile.

"I can tell."

"Live music I don't have to provide."

He draped an arm around her shoulders as they walked. "People expect you to play all the time?"

She rolled her eyes. "You have no idea. I get requests from people I barely know who want me to play at their wedding."

"Beneath you?"

"Oh, no. Nothing like that, but they expect me to play for free, or maybe for dinner."

He chuckled. "Now, I feel guilty."

She looked at him. "Why?"

"I've been trying to figure out where I can find a piano so I can talk you into playing for me."

"You have not."

"I have. I swear. Maybe someday?"

"I would love to play for you, Sawyer."

He squeezed her shoulders and released her to climb on his bike.

Traffic heading to the local amphitheater was heavy and slow. The only question was whether it was cars headed for the concert or headed home after a long holiday weekend. He hoped the cars represented people leaving the area. Not that he minded people. He didn't. But he looked forward to taking Ana on Lakefront Circle without a line of red brake lights ahead, or taking a hike along the lake without a million other people with the same idea, or getting her out on the lake and teaching her how to fish.

When it came to time with Ana, he was a selfish bastard. He knew it and was okay with it. He wanted her all to himself for whatever time they had left.

Life loved to throw curveballs, to shake up the status quo. Meeting Ana had certainly been the rock thrown into his life that he needed, even if he hadn't realized how much his life needed to change. Change might not be the right word. Evolve was more like it. At his age, most men were either settled down with one woman, or were looking for that special person. He'd never given settling down much thought. Like a leaf in a stream, he'd floated along year after year, not worried with where he was headed. Now, that floating leaf had smashed up to Ana-the-boulder in his stream, and he was stuck.

She hugged him tightly as they rode.

Yeah, maybe he didn't mind being the leaf stuck to the boulder.

CHAPTER 8

A na loved being on the back of Sawyer's bike. She knew all about the risks of riding a motorcycle. Besides hearing her mother tell her only uncouth people and troublemakers rode motorcycles, she could hear Randall screeching she could get hurt or break her hands. Maybe, but that didn't stop her from tightening her hold around his waist.

Man, she loved how firm he felt, heck, how secure she felt holding on to him. She felt invincible, even if realistically she knew she was reacting like an adolescent teen. She'd never had time for boys, not really. School work and piano had defined her life.

But Sawyer wasn't a boy, was he? He was a man, and she could honestly say, the first real man she'd ever kissed. Those kisses on her porch had been a total wow, like knocked-her-socks-off incredible. Obviously, he had much more experience with kissing. She couldn't begin to imagine what he would be like in bed.

That thought stunned her. Bed? Sex? She hadn't

given sex any thought outside of scoffing at the love scenes in books. She'd been with two different guys in her life and never had she felt anything like what romance books described. But after Sawyer's talented mouth and tongue, she was beginning to question everything. If she'd misjudged kissing so horribly, maybe sex was more than what she'd experienced...?

Before she could finish all her musing, Sawyer pulled into a gravel lot and roared past cars toward the front. He nuzzled his bike in a small area not far from the amphitheater entrance. As soon as the bike stopped moving, he dropped his feet to the ground and stood.

"Easier to park, right?"

She laughed and climbed off the back. "Much. Plus, we're practically parked at our seats." She pulled the helmet off her head. "How bad's the hair?" she asked as she tried to tame the tangles.

He dropped the kickstand and joined her to remove his helmet. "It's not bad."

He ran his large hand down the back of her head. She shivered in response.

"Your hair is always gorgeous," he said, and leaned over.

She rose on her toes to meet his mouth. He tasted like mint toothpaste and beer. Those two flavors shouldn't have gone together and yet strangely did.

He draped his arm around her shoulders and they headed toward the entrance. She loved how he was always touching her. A stroke of her hair. A fingertip to her knee. A heavy, muscular arm pulling her tight against him. She could get used to that.

Their seats were in the middle of the of the twentieth row. With the way the rows dropped in front of them down to the stage, their view was ideal. Plus, their location made the acoustics excellent…if country music was your jam. Apparently, it was for Sawyer as she heard him singing along with the band, Molly and the Moonshiners, a country cover band who played all the hits of other country musicians. Some of the songs she recognized, but not enough to know the words or much of the melody. Still, having Sawyer's deep alto voice in her ear made the evening pass much too quickly. She whistled and clapped along with the rest of the audience as they demanded an encore from the band.

She knew what that felt like…the demand to reappear and play another piece. Most nights, she was happy to give the audience another musical piece, especially if they'd been receptive and polite during the main performance. But there were those times when dragging herself back on stage was like dragging a mule that didn't want to be moved.

After the second encore song, the band waved and left the stage for the last time.

"Did you have fun?" Sawyer asked, a bright grin on his face.

He rested the palm of his hand on her lower back as they made their way to the exit. The heat from his hand warmed her back and stirred the butterflies in her stomach into flight.

"Yes. Did you know you have a wonderful singing voice?"

His gaze dipped to the ground and the back to her face. "Thank you. I love to sing, but I don't get a lot of chances to belt one out, except for nights like this."

"I suppose singing on the job is taboo for you."

He chuckled. "Yeah, pretty much."

"What about karaoke? Ever do that?"

He laughed again. "My team would never let me live it down if I did."

"Too bad there isn't a karaoke bar around here. That would be fun. I'd love to hear you sing more."

His hand slid up her spine and back down. "Now, you're just being nice."

"No, I'm not. I really like your voice. Do you play the guitar or anything while singing?"

He wiggled his fingers. "I have five thumbs when it comes to musical instruments. I tried the guitar, the trumpet, and even the drums. I love music, but when it comes to producing it, you don't want me on your team. Were you always good on the piano?"

"Yep." They stepped up to his Harley. "To be continued," she said, slipping the helmet over her head.

He climbed on after her, and they slowly made their way among all the cars out of the parking area. She held on tight as he weaved in and out of the line of cars, making his way to the exit before most of the cars they'd been parked around.

Cool evening air flowed around her as Sawyer goosed the gas and the bike shot out onto the highway. The return to Harbin's Harbor was on a fairly empty street. Either the traffic was behind them or the tourist traffic had departed for home. It would be interesting to see what the lake looked like in the morning without all the Labor Day boats and jet skis.

Once back at Harbin's and walking toward their individual cabins, Sawyer laced his fingers through hers. "It's not too late. Want to share a drink and look at the moon?"

"Yes. I don't have any beer or bourbon, but I can offer you wine," she said.

"Give me a couple of minutes to grab my bourbon and a glass. I'll be right back," he said as they stopped at the stairs leading to her porch.

"I have a glass," she said with a smile. "Bring the bourbon and yourself. That's enough."

He grinned, and then kissed her. She leaned into the kiss, not wanting it to be so short. When he broke the kiss to run to his cabin, she almost fell over.

"Be right back," he said, and gave her another kiss.

Ana went inside to pour herself a merlot. There were no wine glasses in the cabin. Only eight-ounce glasses and coffee mugs. She filled a hefty portion of merlot into a glass and got an extra one for Sawyer's bourbon. When she got back to the porch, Sawyer was already waiting.

"Wow. That was fast. Teleportation?"

He chuckled. "Something like that. I didn't want you to change your mind and decide it was too late."

"No way." She jabbed a thumb toward her chest. "This girl is up for a party."

He arched a brow. "Really?"

"Yep. I bet I can stay awake until midnight."

He laughed as he took the glass she offered. After splashing a healthy portion into the glass, he set the bottle on the floor. He held up his glass. "To Molly and the Moonshiners."

Ana tapped her glass to his and took a long sip. "This is really good. I don't drink a lot of wine, or really alcohol, but you introduced me to this brand of merlot, and I love it." She leaned over as though imparting a secret. "I got directions to the winery in Napa. Shh. It could be the next place I run off to."

"My lips are sealed."

They drank for a minute, and then he said, "We

were talking about your piano. When did you start playing?"

"I was about three or four. I would hear a tune and then try to find the right keys to produce the sound. I begged for piano lessons when I was about five. Mom thought I was too young. I disagreed then, and I still do. She should've found me a teacher as soon as I showed the talent and interest."

"Maybe the lessons were a strain on your parents' budget. I mean, piano lessons are a luxury for a lot of families."

She realized he had no idea about her family…all the ridiculous money her grandparents had, all the millions her mother had.

Before she could respond, he said, "Wait. I just realized your family had a piano when you were little. Otherwise, you wouldn't have been picking out tunes, right?"

She nodded. "We had an older piano that nobody played. Mom inherited it from her grandmother, so it was more of a sentimental keepsake."

"So, your mother didn't play?"

She shook her head. "Nor my father."

"Your grandparents? Did you inherit your talent from your mother's side or your dad's side?"

"My great-grandmother. She taught piano lessons to help make ends meet." She wasn't lying. Her mother's grandparents had had nothing until their son hit it big in real estate. Now, her family had money flowing like an open faucet.

"That probably makes your mom and your grandparents happy that her talent was passed along."

Actually, it didn't. Her grandmother felt Ana having a career was ridiculous since her trust fund was large enough to pay for anything and everything Ana might want, as well as any children she might have. Her grandmother grudgingly accepted her piano playing because it was the classics and not some pop nonsense. However, she'd rather Ana had fulfill her role in Chicago society.

"I'm sure they are," she lied.

"I hate to bring this up, but you've been missing since Friday. They must be worried about you. Don't you think you should let them know you're okay?"

"If I call home with my cell, the location of the call will be recorded. If Randall knew I was this close to San Diego, he would be here in hours to guilt me into going back, and frankly, I'm not ready to go back." She looked at him. "I'm exhausted, Sawyer. Not physically, but mentally. I needed to read some romance novels and eat some taboo foods, and maybe kiss a sexy man. I'm not ready to give all that up."

"So, call home on my phone. I can block the number so it will read 'private' on their end. You can tell them anything you want to, but they need to know you're okay."

She nodded. "You're probably right. It's too late tonight. But since you offered, I'll use your phone to call my parents' housephone. Someone will answer, and I can let them know I'm fine." She looked at him. "Thanks. Seems like this is the second time you've come to my rescue when I needed help."

He reached over and took her hand. "I'm glad I could be here for you." He studied her face for a long while, and then said, "I really like you, Ana. You're funny, and easy to talk to, and so, so sexy. You sort of blow me away."

Her eyes opened wide. "You think I'm sexy?"

"Oh, babe. You rock my boat like no one ever has."

Heat flushed up her neck and to her cheeks. Her gaze dropped to the porch. "I know what you mean." She looked up at him. "You're like no man I've ever known. You're kind of blowing me away, too."

"Whew. Glad to know I'm not in this by myself."

"Nope. I'm right there with you." She stood, walked over to where he sat, and leaned down. "I've never initiated a kiss before."

"Hey, no time like the present."

The smile on his face and the twinkle in his eyes were all the encouragement she needed. She leaned down and pressed her lips to his. He let her drive the kiss, and that shook her to her bones. She had no idea what she was doing. Still, she put her hand on either side of his face and found his beard soft to the touch. She'd already noticed that earlier when he kissed her, but now, her fingers spread and glided through his velvety facial hair.

After her second tentative kiss, Sawyer pulled her onto his lap. "I love how merlot tastes on your lips. Now, let's see how it tastes on your tongue." When he spoke, his lips touched hers with each word. His voice, deep and rough, sent chills up and down her back like he was playing scales on her spine.

He angled his head and gave her a deep, soul-crushing kiss. She opened her lips readily for him, meeting his tongue with hers as he thrust into her mouth. The kiss was all tongue and lips and heat. Her stomach squeezed. The area behind her navel pulled. Tingles and hotness hit between her thighs with a force she'd never felt.

Her arms weaved around his neck. Her body pressed against his as though she was trying to get inside his chest. She groaned and rubbed her aching nipples against his hard chest, not finding the relief she sought, even if she didn't exactly know what she was seeking.

Sawyer's hand cupped one globe of her rear. His fingers flexed, caressing her bottom in his hand. His mouth left kisses along her cheek then down her neck. Her head fell to the side, exposing more skin that wanted his mouth desperately.

She wiggled on his lap, the ache between her thighs growing exponentially with each thrust of his tongue. Beneath her bottom, she felt Sawyer's cock, hard and thick.

Her hand found the band at the nape of his neck holding his hair. She pulled it out, freeing his long hair for her fingers to stroke. The strands were silky and soft. She loved how they felt gliding between her fingers.

Sawyer breathed into her ear, giving her chill bumps another boost. "God, Ana. You are so fucking sexy," he whispered into her ear. He kissed her there then he ran the tip of his tongue along the top of her ear. "But we have to stop."

"Why?" She pulled away until she could see his face, and what she saw stunned her. His eyes were dilated with lust; his lips were swollen and red from their kisses; his breathing was labored; his hair blowing in all directions from the breeze off the lake and the raking of her fingers. Behind the hand she rested on his chest, his heart pounded rapidly.

Her heart raced and throbbed painfully against her chest. Her lips were probably swollen and red. Her hair was draped over his supporting arm and tossing in the wind. Did her eyes look like his? Was he as turned on as she was?

"You know why," he said. "If we don't stop now, I won't want to stop." He stood, rising to his full height with her in his arms. "I'm going to put you inside your cabin. I want you to shut the door and lock it."

She smiled and kissed him again. He groaned.

"Ana, you're playing with fire, and I don't want you to get burned."

She stuck out her bottom lip in a sulk. He caught her pouting lip between his and sucked. Her breath caught, and she moaned.

"And that's why you're going inside right now," he ordered. Still holding her, he opened her door, set her on her feet inside her living room, sighed loudly, and cussed. Then he shut the door.

"Lock it," he said through the door.

Ana locked the door, then leaned on it and slid to the floor until her knees were bent up to her chest. Her mind whirled. Her lust-addled brain wanted to follow him back to his place, but fear stopped her. Not fear that he'd hurt her or anything like that. Fear that the experience would be like her others, leaving her disappointed. She liked Sawyer too much to risk it.

But it was a long time before she was able to fall asleep.

CHAPTER 9

The next morning, Sawyer knocked on her door. When she opened it, he kissed her, handed her a cup of coffee, and waved as he jogged down the steps.

"I'll be back in a couple of hours. Want to finally do the Lakefront Circle? Maybe go on a hike?"

She took a sip of coffee and nodded. "Sounds perfect. I'll see you later."

He blew a kiss and jogged out of sight.

Ana sagged into a chair on the porch. The sun was still low in the sky. A bright yellow ribbon burned across the water from the base of the sun. Somewhere, a bird chirped happily. A butterfly flittered across her porch, landing momentarily on the railing before taking off again. The scene was almost idyllic. She hated to mess up this perfect picture, but she should probably check her emails while Sawyer was gone. When she'd walked with Sawyer to the office to return his fishing gear, she'd noticed a "business area" with a computer and printer for guests. She'd finish her coffee and get dressed. Then she'd face her dragons.

Mandy was behind the desk in the office when Ana entered.

"Good morning," Mandy said. "Everything okay with the cabin?"

"It's perfect," Ana replied. "This morning, the sun shining across the water was almost too ideal, as though someone painted it just for me."

Mandy smiled. "Aaron and I are so lucky to live here. We talk about it often. What can I do for you today?"

"I wondered if I could use your business area to check my emails?" Ana tilted her head toward the computer and printer in the corner.

"Sure. Help yourself."

"Thanks."

Ana sat and booted up the computer. After opening a web browser, she opened a tab for an incognito window, and closed the original tab. Now, she was supposed to be untraceable online. She guessed that would remain to be seen.

Her inbox was stuffed with over a thousand messages. Of course, many of them had come in before she'd left and she just hadn't felt like dealing with them. However, one that'd come in on Friday did. It was from the Peabody Institute in Baltimore, Maryland. She clicked it first, and gasped as she read. She was being invited to serve as Artist-in-Residence for May of the following year. Stunned, she sat back in her chair. This was incredible. She wondered if Randall had read this yet as he'd been cc'd on the invite. She filed the message in her "invitations" folder and would respond when she returned.

Then she scanned through the long list of messages

from Randall, Geoffrey, and her mother. She started with the earliest ones from last Friday.

Basically, her mother's messages started out with concern. By Sunday's message, she was demanding that Ana call Randall or Geoffrey, which was interesting. Not call home, but call her manager. Yesterday's email from dear old mom was short and curt. *Call Randall or else.* Ana laughed to herself. Or else what? Cut her off?

First, she had a trust fund that would be hers when she turned thirty-three, or got married, whichever came first. The wording in the trust was ironclad and there was nothing her mother could do to change it. Second, she made enough money with her career that money wasn't an issue, making her mother's threat the limp noodle of threats.

Randall's messages began demanding to know where she was when she didn't respond to his email nor answered her phone. By Monday, all his messages were in capital letters, going so far as to threaten to fire her as a client. If that was meant to scare her, it didn't. In fact, she mostly shrugged at the threat. She was more important to him than he was to her, or at least the many offers of representation she'd had from other agents suggested that.

There was one email from Geoffrey that'd arrived on Sunday. It read…

Ana –

I'm not sure where you are, but I'm worried about you. You haven't been yourself lately and of course I noticed. I think I caught you off-guard with my marriage proposal, but I'm not sure why. I've mentioned our being together for the long haul, and I thought you understood what I meant. I want you to know that both my dad and your mom are thrilled by the idea of us marrying. In fact, I'm pretty sure you mom has reserved the Penthouse Restaurant for the Friday before Thanksgiving for our wedding. She's so thoughtful like that.

I know you haven't said yes yet, but we both know getting married makes sense. No one can understand your career with its stresses more than I can. Dad has mentioned that once we are married, he would be happy to let me take over more of your management. Additionally, as Dad will be sixty-five this year, he's talking more about completely retiring after we wed and handing over the company reins. My dad and your mom thought my managing your career as your husband was an excellent idea as I'd have more of an invested interest in your success.

We have been friends for years and I think the best relationships are based on friendship. Love will grow in the right setting, and I'm sure you will come to feel for me what I feel for you. We share a mutual respect for each other and the industry. Marrying our careers makes logical sense. Passion doesn't rule our lives nor our decisions, which is good. Passion will fade after marriage. A friendship is forever.

I understand from your mother that you will come into your trust upon marrying or turning thirty-three. Marrying me in only a couple of months would free up your trust to buy us a home in the building where your parents live. Your mom says there is a condo on the floor just below them, so she thought it would be ideal.

As far as children, I know you'd like a child, and I'm fine with that. However, I think waiting a few years would be the prudent thing to do.

I hope you are away giving my proposal and our life together serious thought.

As your mom told me, your marrying me would be the

*best business decision for your career and she looks forward
to welcoming me as her son-in-law.*

Fondly,

Geoffrey

Ana leaned back in her chair, stunned and angry.
How dare her mom accept a marriage proposal *for her*,
and then have the audacity to reserve a venue for a
wedding that would never happen. The idea of being
married to Geoffrey made her throw up a little in her
mouth. The idea of kissing him like she had Sawyer
made her nauseous. And sex? Lord help. She suspected
he had a penis, but she also suspected his father
controlled it.

And marrying him being the best career decision?
Her mom probably did say that. After all, her mom had
discouraged Ana from dating in college, pushing her
to focus on what was more important than any relationship…her piano.

Still, the idea of Geoffrey Blagg as her husband
was, well, unthinkable. She liked Geoffrey and they
were friends, but beyond that? Nope.

Her problem was she knew the kind of pressure
Randall and her mother would put on her as soon as
she resurfaced, and she suspected they were already
applying the same pressure to Geoffrey. Sadly, Ana
had a history of giving into them. Not this time, she
vowed.

The next email was a complete surprise. She hadn't
even known her father had an email address.

Hello Kitten

Her heart melted a little. Her dad had always called
her Kitten, to her mother's displeasure. Sometimes,
Ana wondered if that's why he kept it up all her life.

I've heard the screams and rants of frustration from

*your mom with your "unscheduled vacation," but after so
many years, I've gotten used to them. What I haven't gotten
used to, and never will, is not talking to you. I don't know
where you ran off to, and I don't care. All I care about is
that you're safe and having some fun, for once in your life. I
will never win Father of the Year, but I will always love you
and want what is best for you.*

*Now, having said all that, I am hearing discussions
about you marrying Randall's son, Geoffrey. I have no
objection IF you love him. Marriage has its ups and its
downs. Without love, life as a couple would be miserable.
And before you question me, yes, I love your mother. She
was the most dazzling woman I'd ever met. Sophisticated.
Classy. I knew her family had money, but that never meant
a thing to me. I wanted her. Of course, you are aware that
she was pregnant with you when we married. Her parents
were furious. They had picked out a more suitable man for
her. I was not their choice, but I'm sure none of that is a
surprise to you. The minute I saw you, all red and crying in
the delivery room, I knew what love was, but I also knew
what fear was. I knew I always had to be there for you. I
hope I have been.*

*Back to marrying Geoffrey. Ask yourself these
questions.*

*Does your heart pound when you see him? Does your
breath catch when you look at him? Does your stomach have
butterflies around him?*

*Does he make you laugh? Has he made your cry?
Laughing is good. Crying is not.*

*Does he make you feel like you're the center of his
world? Do you feel special when you are around him? Do
you feel safe? Do you feel like he would protect you from the
rest of the world? Does he stand with you against the world?
Do you feel like he's the one and only for you?*

Do you trust him? Not just with your heart, but with all your secrets too?

Does he put you first?

I'm your father, so I'll pretend you know nothing about sex, but does he make you swoon? Do you hate when the night ends and you have to go separate ways? Do his kisses make you question all the men who came before him?

This is how I felt about your mom. I knew from the moment I met her. There were no questions for me that she was the one I wanted, even if she did come with parents from hell. (Don't tell your grandmother I said that! On the other hand, she's never thought I was good enough for her daughter, so to hell with her! Tell her anything you want. Ha!)

If you don't feel this way about Geoffrey, don't marry him.

I know your mother thinks this is the perfect solution, you marrying the son of your manager, but I'm not sure. I've not voiced my concerns to your mom since you know that once she gets her mind set on something, she won't let it go.

If you come back and you don't want to marry Geoffrey, I will stand with you on this.

If you come back and you want to marry Geoffrey, I will proudly walk you down the aisle.

But be sure, Kitten.

I love you.

Dad

Ana wiped a tear from her eye. Her father had never talked to her like this. He'd always let her mother drive their marriage, but now she thought she understood why. Her father loved her mother. It was a shocking revelation.

She hit reply for the first time today.

Dad

Your words meant a lot to me. I'm safe. I'm fine. I'd rather not say where I am, but I'm relaxing and enjoying every day. I'll be home soon.

Love

Ana

Sawyer had been right about her checking in. She needed to call home and let them know she was fine, but needed a little time alone.

"You okay?" Mandy asked from the desk.

Ana wiped her cheeks with the back of her hand and sniffed. "Yeah, I'm okay."

"It's not Sawyer, is it? He hasn't done something to upset you, has he? I mean, I don't know him well, but he's been coming here for a couple of years and seems like a decent guy."

Ana looked over at Mandy and smiled. "Not Sawyer. He's kind of perfect, you know?"

Mandy chuckled. "Well, don't let my husband hear me say this, but whew." She waved a hand in front of her face. "You should see him without all the facial hair. Dreamy."

"He's pretty dreamy with it," Ana said with a grin.

"That's true. Did you two have fun last night at the concert?"

"Gosh, yes. Did you and your husband go?"

"Of course. I never miss Molly and the Moon-shiners when they're in town."

"Local group?"

"More like a California group. They travel up and down the state and have developed quite a following. Want a water or something while you work?"

Ana closed the web browse window and stood.

"Thanks, but no. I'm done for now. Appreciate your letting me use the computer."

"Sure. Anytime. The cabin working out okay?"

"Perfect, thanks."

"Well, if you need anything, just give me shout."

Sawyer was jogging into the parking lot as she exited the office.

"Hey, beautiful," he said. He slowed and jogged in place. "You wouldn't know of a sexy woman who'd like to go for a bike ride this afternoon, do you?"

Ana's heart leapt. Her breath caught in her throat. A million butterflies launched themselves in her stomach. The palms of her hands began to sweat.

She smiled at this gorgeous man, this perfect man, standing in front of her. "I think I might. Check cabin ten for a passenger volunteer."

He laughed, his white teeth flashing in the bright sun. "I hear there's a real hottie staying there." He pumped his eyebrows. "Think she'd be interested in a hot, sweaty SEAL?"

She swallowed against the lump that formed in her throat. Hot, sweaty and sexy. "Hmm. She might be. Want me to walk with you to ask her?" She stepped up to him and lifted her face for a kiss.

He didn't hesitate to lean down and kiss her. He tasted salty, but even then, she thought him the best thing that'd happen to her in a long time.

"I suggest a shower first," she said with a grin.

"What? You think I smell? C'mon here closer." He reached out for her, the sweat on his arms glistening.

She laughed and danced away. "No way. I've had my shower, and I don't want a second one."

He leered at her. She giggled and took off running toward her cabin, Sawyer on her heels. Of course, he could catch her without much effort on his part. Still, he played her game and chased her all the way back to cabin ten.

"Well, if you're going to be that way," he said as she bolted up the stairs to her porch. "I'm going to go take a shower alone. I would've invited you along, but not now...that you've hurt my sensitive feelings." He pulled his mouth into a frown and sniffled.

She laughed. "Go. Shower. I need to take Barbie down for her new shoes. Maybe you could pick me up and we could do Lakefront Circle today?"

"That sounds like a great plan."

They spent Tuesday riding around the lake, stopping from time to time to take in the views and admire the large, impressive houses along the lakefront. They found a small grocery-slash-deli on the far side of the lake and picked up a couple of sandwiches, chips, and soft drinks.

Sawyer talked her into hiking up a trail to an overlook to eat lunch. While she playfully moaned the whole way, Sawyer laughed and pushed her to keep up with him. But she was fully aware he could leave her in the dust on the hike if he'd wanted to.

And that was a huge difference between Sawyer and Geoffrey.

Sawyer encouraged her, which motivated her. Geoffrey thought he was motivating her to do better when he pointed out all her faults and errors. That didn't inspire her. Those comments only angered her.

But, in Geoffrey's defense, he'd learned that from his father, who'd pushed Geoffrey to develop his piano skills. Unfortunately, Geoffrey didn't have the musical talent to take his piano aptitude beyond mid-grade professional. He would never reach Ana's proficiency level, which was somewhat of a sore point for him. He swore he didn't care, but she didn't believe that for one minute. No one practiced as long and as hard as he did if they "didn't care" about improving. He'd reached his pinnacle in his twenties. Now, at forty, he had to make himself content with the occasional performance on a local stage and the stream of students who wanted to learn from him. He was an excellent teacher, but sadly, teaching didn't fulfill him professionally and probably never would.

Sawyer and Ana spent the afternoon riding around and just enjoying the sights, and each other. He got a call from Billy Bob in the late afternoon to tell Ana her car was ready. Sawyer took her over and waited while she wrote a check for the new-slash-used tires. She worried he wouldn't take a check since so many places wouldn't these days, but he was happy to take hers, pleased to avoid the credit card fee.

Once they were back at the cabin, Ana knew she had to call home. She trusted him when he'd said he could protect her from anyone learning her location.

"Sawyer?" She looked over at him. His hair was tied back. He was lifting a glass of bourbon to his lips.

He paused the glass and said, "Yes?"

She sighed. "When I was coming out of the office today, I'd been checking my emails."

His brows rose. "Is that why you looked unhappy this afternoon?" He frowned. "What'd they say? Whose ass do I need to go kick?"

With a chuckle, she said, "Down, boy. No ass-kicking needed, at least, not right now. My manager and my mom are pretty livid."

"Screw 'em. You're an adult."

"I know, but you know how family pressure is, or

maybe you don't." She grinned. "You did join the Navy after all."

"I do know about family pressure." He turned toward her. "What do you need? What can I do to help?"

"I need to call home to at least let my parents know I'm okay. You said I could use your phone."

He pulled his cell phone from his pocket and punched a few keys. "There. When you call, the number will show as restricted or maybe private. Anyway, they won't have a way to call back." He handed her the phone. "I'm going to walk up to the office to give you some privacy and have something delivered for dinner. What about Italian?"

"Italian sounds good," Her stomach was in nervous knots. She wondered if she'd be able to swallow any food. And if she did, would it stay down?

"Chin up," he said, taking her chin between his thumb and forefinger. "You've got this." He kissed her and left.

She stared at the phone in her shaking hand. Sawyer was right. She was an adult fully in charge of her life...starting now.

She dialed her parents' landline and waited as it rang. On the third ring, the phone was answered.

"Cristiano residence," the accented voice of their housekeeper said.

"Lulu?"

"Ana? Oh, baby. Are you okay? Your parents are out of their minds with worry."

"I'm fine. I just needed some time away. Is Dad there?" she asked then added, "or Mom?"

"No, honey. They're both out right now. Give me a number. I'm sure they'll want to call you back."

"No, that's okay. Just let them know I called, and I'm fine. Actually, I'm more than fine. I'm having a wonderful vacation in…New York City. Doing some shopping. Got a massage. Ate some great food."

"Well, that sounds wonderful. I know they'll be sorry to have missed your call. Your mom is all excited about your getting married in November. That's where she is now. She's visiting bridal salons, looking for the perfect dress."

Ana rolled her eyes while at the same time, gritting her teeth. Her mother could infuriate her. Talk about overstepping her bounds.

"You know Mom loves to shop. I'd better run. I've got an, um, manicure scheduled in fifteen minutes. Tell them I'm sorry I missed them, but I'll be in touch later."

She clicked off with a sigh of relief. One bullet dodged. She'd called home as requested. It wasn't her fault her mother was out *shopping for bridal gowns*! Sawyer, bless his heart, had no idea the kind of pressure that'd be put on her to marry Geoffrey when she got back. She had nothing against Geoffrey. It was that she felt nothing for him except professional courtesy.

If she called Randall, would Sawyer's phone still be masked, or did that undo after one call? She didn't have a clue. On the other hand, she didn't want to talk to Randall, so not knowing about masking the phone was excuse enough, in her humble opinion. Besides, her mother would call Randall as soon as Lulu told her about Ana's call.

She lifted her wine glass to her mouth and drew in a long gulp. Getting that call over with had taken a load off her shoulders. Now, she could relax and have a nice meal with a sexy man.

CHAPTER 10

S awyer was awake before the sun broke the horizon. Typically, he could sleep anywhere, and he didn't need much sleep to function. But last night, when he'd returned from ordering Italian for dinner, Ana's mood had been lighter than it had been all day.

She'd handed him his phone with a polite, "Thank you," and that was it. No mention of the call, or even who she'd called. But whatever had happened during his absence had put her in a good mood.

He rolled over in bed and let the memories from last night roll through his head. Dinner, wine, and then she'd invited him inside to, "Get away from the mosquitoes." Now, he hadn't seen a mosquito their entire stay, but he'd followed her inside to her living room. There, the hottest make-out session he'd had since high school took place on her sofa. At one point, he'd been on top of her, his cock so hard it hurt, and it had taken every ounce of willpower not to strip her bare right there and take her. God knew he wanted her…bad. He ached to know what it would feel like as he thrust deep inside her. He'd kill to know what she sounded like when she came. And if he didn't get to taste the sweetness of her arousal, he might go insane.

His cock stiffened at the memories. No woman had ever driven him to this point of desperation before.

His hand wrapped around his cock and stroked. Blood rushed down, making his dick as hard as a rock. He moved his hand faster, sliding it from base to tip in a frenzy to relieve the ache. With Ana on his mind, the memory of the taste of her lips prominent in his thoughts, it didn't take but a few strokes before he felt the tug at the base of his spine. His balls drew up, ready to spill him into his sheets.

He came with a groan, the ache for Ana lessened but far from being placated. Only the real woman would do.

Checking the time on his phone, he saw it was early, plenty of time to get in his run before he and Ana were scheduled to pick up the pontoon boat he'd reserved for today. Mandy was also holding fishing gear for both of them. All that was missing was a swim suit for Ana. She wanted to swim, so he'd promised to make a stop on the way to the marina so she could buy one. He held out hope for a very tiny bikini. Of course, Ana in a barely-there bikini might be the best thing that'd ever happened to him, or might be the thing that would drive him over the edge. Only time would tell.

He did his morning run, fully aware that he cut a couple of miles off. He was impatient to get back to the cabin and see if Ana was awake.

To his pleasure, she was sitting in her usual place on her porch, Ranger laying at her feet and looking at her with adoring eyes. It might have been Ana herself who had the dog in a thrall, or it might have been the bagel in her hand. Either way, Ranger was not moving.

"Good morning," he said, leaning on her railing.

She smiled, and he felt his heart shift.

"Good morning. I see you got your run done already."

"Yep. Were you planning on going with me today?" He'd invited her every day, and every day, she'd demurred.

"I was," she said brightly. She snapped her fingers. "Too bad I missed it." Then her cheeky grin gave her away.

"Right," he said with a laugh. "Tomorrow's another day."

"That's right. And you know what tomorrow is!"

He frowned and pretended to think. "Um, Thursday?" When she shot him a glare, he laughed. "Your birthday. I couldn't forget that. Leaving the neurotic twenties behind and officially moving into the self-confident thirties."

"Self-confident thirties. I like how that sounds. What time are we leaving? Don't forget I need to pick up a swimsuit on the way."

"I haven't forgotten. I'll jump in the shower and be right back." He stepped back and stopped. "And don't feed Ranger anything. He's fat and spoiled and doesn't need a thing."

She gasped and leaned over to run her hand alone Ranger's head. "Don't listen to the mean, mean man. In fact, go bite him."

Ranger's tongue lolled out of his mouth, and he licked Ana's hand as though to say, "I love you, Ana. Can I have a bite of bagel?"

Sawyer rolled his eyes and hurried to his cabin, albeit with a huge grin.

They opted to take Barbie to the marina, mostly because Sawyer wanted to make sure the alignment was good and the ride smooth. On the way, he dropped Ana at a beach boutique while he ran to pick up the snacks and drinks for the day on the lake. He would have loved to have gone shopping with Ana, but she wanted to surprise him, or that's what she'd said.

He finished with his shopping before she did, so he parked the Malibu in front of the store to wait. He was content waiting for her. In so many ways, he felt like he'd waited for her his whole life. He scrolled through emails and texts that'd accrued over the past couple of days. Nothing urgent. His parents were enjoying Belgium and wished he could have gone with them. He wished his parents were here to meet Ana. Of course, it was only their cancellation of their trip to Lake Kincade that had opened up the cabin for Ana.

Fate sure was playing matchmaker, not that he was complaining. However, the rate at which he'd fallen for Ana was disquieting. He was pretty sure it had happened the minute she'd wrapped her arms around his legs on the roller coaster, putting all her trust into him. Or maybe he'd fallen during the miniature golf game. Or the race cars. He'd loved her excitement.

Oh, who was he kidding? He'd fallen like Humpty Dumpty off his wall the minute he'd laid eyes on Ana with Ranger on Saturday morning. Splat, and it was all over for him.

But last night's long talk and make-out session had sealed the deal for him. He wanted this woman. He knew she was out of his league. More educated. Probably smarter. Definitely better looking and sexier than any woman he'd ever known. Crazy, but back when he'd seen her play in Germany and they'd just been kids, it'd been like seeing his future. The truth was, he'd long given up trying to find that girl from his childhood. Heck, he'd thought her name had been Anna. But now fate had given him a second chance to grab the brass ring. He only had to make a dangerous lean from his comfort zone to reach for it without crashing and burning.

The passenger door opened. "I'm here," Ana said, slipping into the car. She tossed a shopping bag into the back seat.

"Did you find a suit?"

"I did."

He frowned. "Where is it? Are you going to change on the boat?" Not that he would mind at all.

She laughed. "I'm wearing it."

He studied the shorts and the Lake Kincade T-Shirt she wore, which was not what she'd had on when she'd entered the store. "You're planning on swimming in a T-shirt and shorts?

She laughed again. "No, silly. It's on under my clothes." She hitched a thumb toward the back. "My clothes are in the bag. I wore my new things out." She pointed to her temple. "Smart, right?"

"Definitely. I was just thinking that you were probably smarter than I am."

With a scoff and an eyeroll, she said, "Doubt it. I have more education in music, but that's about it. I bet you know how to pick locks or build a bomb or something. I could never do anything like that."

He started the car and glanced over at her. "I have so many skills I can teach you." And he didn't mean bombs and guns.

She arched a brow. "Oh, really? This day just got a whole lot more interesting." Then she giggled. "Let's go. I bet besides bombs and guns, you know something about boats."

"A thing or two."

At Medlin Marine, good news and bad news awaited them.

"Sorry, man," the manager said. "My son double-booked the sixteen-foot pontoon boats, and the twenty-foot boats." He shook his head. "Knucklehead. There's probably a girl in a bikini that explains it. So that's the bad news for us. The good news for you is that I have a twenty-six-foot unit that I'll rent you for the same price as the sixteen-foot you reserved."

Sawyer grinned. "You know bikinis make us guys do crazy things."

The manager laughed. "Oh, yes. I remember my younger days. So that works for you? You can handle the bigger boat?"

"No problem. Been boating forever." Sawyer handed the man a credit card. While he rang the charge, Sawyer filled out the required paperwork and handed over his driver's license and military identification.

After the manager made copies of Sawyer's identification and returned them, he set a key on a spiral stretch keychain on the counter. "Boat is in slot twelve. If my son hasn't fallen in the lake, he'll help you get it untied and out of the slip."

Twenty minutes after they'd parked Barbie, Sawyer and Ana were on a new pontoon boat and backing it out into the lake. As soon as they cleared the dock and were headed into open waters, Sawyer pulled his shirt off and tossed it to Ana.

"Stash that somewhere so I won't lose it." When she didn't say anything, he looked at her. She was studying him like he was a lab experience. "What? What's wrong?"

"Wow," she said. "I, um, well, wow."

As her gaze ran up and down his chest, his skin heated like she was shooting lasers. Nothing like a gorgeous woman drooling over his chest to make him want to puff it out.

"You like what you see?"

"I understand why Mandy asked you to wear a shirt while running to avoid causing traffic jams and accidents."

He laughed. "She was kidding."

Ana slowly shook her head. "I don't think so." She leaned over until her finger tips touched his tattoo. "I like this. It's very sexy."

"It's the Navy SEAL insignia."

Her fingers traced the tattoo, which felt like it was on fire from her simple touch. "I saw the bottom of the anchor once. I couldn't figure out the gun until today. Did it hurt?"

"Not too much."

"Your only tattoo?"

He shook his head and turned to show her the frog outline with a trident tattoo on his right chest pec. "That's all for now. I've been thinking of getting one on my back."

"What would you put there?" she asked as she continued to stroke his arm.

"Not sure yet. How many tattoos do you have?"

She burst out laughing. "Can you imagine what my mother or Randall would say if I got a tattoo?"

He shook his head. "Actually, I can't. I don't know either of them."

"Well, my mother would immediately start calling all the dermatologists in Chicago to book the best one known for tattoo removal. Randall would faint."

"You know, honey, they can't control your life if you don't let them."

A frown wrinkled her brow as she scooted back onto her seat. "Let's ride around for a while. I want to look at all the fancy houses."

Well, she'd shut down that conversation. He wasn't sure what thought went through her head just then, but whatever it was, it hadn't been a pleasant one.

"But first…" Ana said.

Sawyer looked over in time to watch her pull the Lake Kincade T-shirt over her head and store it with his. He gulped. Holy shit. The tiny jade-green bikini top barely covered her breasts. In fact, the material seemed to be perched over her nipples and that was about it.

When she stood and tucked her thumbs into the waistband of her shorts to pull those down, he thought his heart might stop. Nope. Not stopped. Instead, it galloped around his chest and pounded painfully against his ribs. Dear lord. She was stunning. Mouth-gaping, drool-producing, stunningly gorgeous.

Her breasts were round and perfect. Her figure cut in at her waist and flared out again at her hips. He'd known she had great legs, but he'd only seen them from about the knees down. Now, fully exposed to his gaze, he could see her thighs were as shapely as her calves. His cock stiffened and strained against the material confining it.

"Um, the boat?" she said. "You might want to look where you're driving?"

"What? Oh!" He glanced forward, saw nothing but open water, then turned back to her. "Good God, Ana." He ran his gaze from her toes to her eyes—which were sparkling—back down to her hips. "That suit is..."

"Nice? Pretty?" she suggested.

"Giving me a heart attack," he said. "Whew. Woman. Get over here and kiss me."

He stopped the boat in the middle of the wide main channel as she stepped over to where he sat in the captain's chair. He ran his hands along her hips and traced the very thin cord that connected the front and back of the sunshine yellow triangle of material barely covering her sex. His fingers slipped under the material in the back and stroked the soft globes of her ass.

She smiled and ran her hands up his chest to encircle his neck.

He rotated the chair and pulled her until she sat straddling his aching cock. She pressed her crotch against his rock-hard, and painful dick.

"Damn, woman," he said. "You are so fucking sexy."

He fisted one hand into her hair and jerked her toward him. The kiss was hungry and desperate. He thrust his tongue inside her hot mouth like he wanted to thrust his cock into her hot pussy. Her tongue met his, more forceful than the first time she'd tasted him.

Her fingers loosened the band holding back his hair and threaded through his strands. Like he'd done to her hair, her hands fisted and she pulled his hair with a groan and a grind of her pussy against his cock. The hand inside her suit bottom found the crack between her ass cheeks and he slid a finger downward.

"Oh, God," she said against his lips.

A passing boat tooted its horn as a group of college-aged couples passed. "Find a cove," one of them yelled. The group laughed, while the guys all held thumbs up.

"Wow. I might have just lost my mind," she said and stood.

Her face was flushed. Her hair was a tangled, knotted mess. Her eyes were heavy with lust.

"I haven't lost mine," he said. "I want you, Ana. I want you in every way possible. I want to make love to you. I want to taste you, mark you with my teeth. Spend an entire night doing nothing but touching you."

She gasped in a breath.

"But," he continued, "I don't think you're ready for that." He sighed and tossed his hair over his shoulders. "Let's go for that ride before I explode with lust. Sit."

He faced forward and gave the motor gas. The boat shot forward, and he heard Ana drop onto the seat across from him.

For the next ten minutes or so, he drove, his cock getting the message that nothing was happening. He purposely took them to an area of multi-million-dollar estates in an attempt to take both of their minds off a kiss that had almost had him coming in his shorts, something he hadn't done in twenty years.

"Look at that one," he said, pointing to a Spanish-style mansion on a hill. "You like that one?"

He chanced a glance in her direction.

She smiled and stood. Walking behind him, she draped her arms around his neck and let them dangle in front of his chest. "Thank you," she said into his ear. "No one has ever made me feel like you do. I'm sorry I got embarrassed. I'm not used to men wanting me."

"No, babe. Trust me. Every man who sees you wants you. I'm just the lucky fool who was in the right place at the right time to get your attention." He pulled her left hand to his mouth and kissed her fingers. When she started to remove her arms, he said, "No, stay. I like having you close."

"Perfect. I like being close."

At twenty-thousand acres, Lake Kincade had miles of shoreline to explore and hundreds of mansions and estates to see from the water. What he discovered was her wicked sense of humor as she critiqued the estates. She knew not only music, but apparently had an excellent working knowledge of architecture. She could point out the mistakes or problems she could see with the structures themselves or sometimes the gardens. Her funniest caustic remarks were saved for the over-the-top pools with their waterfalls and cascades. He was thoroughly entertained. If she hadn't captured his heart before today, she would have now.

At close to noon, he pulled into a secluded cove and dropped anchor. "I'm starved. Are you ready for lunch? Please say yes."

She chuckled. "I would love to eat something. I didn't have much breakfast."

He chuffed. "You should've said something sooner."

She patted her flat belly. "You've kept me fed like a turkey being fattened for Thanksgiving."

With a scoff, he said, "Seriously? You have no belly."

She turned sideways. "See?"

"No. What I see is a healthy, beautiful woman I've become crazy about."

She grinned. "Don't start that. You know I'll end up in your lap again and look what happened last time."

With a long, exasperated sigh, he nodded. "It's getting warm. Want to swim after lunch?"

"Yes." Her voice was enthusiastic.

He raised an eyebrow. "I worry that suit will dissolve in the water. There's already so little of it."

She giggled as she turned her back to him and leaned over to dig through the ice chest of drinks. The back of her bottoms rode up into her crack, leaving both ass cheeks exposed. His gaze ate up the vision in front of him. Damnation.

"You're playing with fire, honey. You know that?"

Still leaning from her waist, she glanced back at him. "Hmm?" Then she grinned. "You've already felt them," she said with a shrug. "Thought you'd like to see them."

He gave out a strangled chuckle. "You're killing me."

"But what a nice way to die...?" she asked. Then her eyes shut, and she shook her head. "I don't know what has gotten into me. I never talk like that."

He grabbed her around her waist and pulled her back to his chest. "I like it, you sexy girl."

"Today, I shall be a woman."

He laughed, kissed her ear, and reached around her for a Mountain Dew.

They ate deli sandwiches with soft drinks. All the while, he tried to ignore the powerful pull he felt toward this woman.

After lunch, Ana said, "Show me how SEALs go into the water."

Since he was already wearing his swimming trucks, he climbed onto the boat's railing. "Like this." He flopped backwards into the deep water.

She laughed and clapped. "Now, show me how you'd jump from a plane."

He shook his wet hair back and climbed the ladder back onto the boat. "From a plane? With or without a parachute?" When she gasped, he added, "I'm kidding, mostly. But I have jumped from a helicopter into the ocean. It looks like this." He climbed on the backseat, stood straight, pretended he was adjusting his mask, stepped up on the rail, and jumped feet first into the water.

Ana clapped and whistled.

"Now," he said from the water. "Show me how a pianist gets into the water."

With a nod, she climbed on the rear seat and executed a perfect shallow, standing dive off the back. She surfaced close to him. "How'd I do?"

"Impressive."

"I took swimming lessons as a kid. My mom was a terrible swimmer, and she wanted to make sure I wasn't."

"Too bad about your mom. Let me grab those float noodles off the boat." He climbed onboard and grabbed the two yellow float noodles. He tossed both of them to her and dove in. He swam up to her legs and wrapped his arms around her thighs.

She shrieked and kicked out. She was laughing when he surfaced. She bopped him over the head with one of the noodles.

He looped the noodle under his arms and floated. She mimicked his position.

"You ever been in love, Sawyer?"

The question caught him off-guard. He wasn't exactly sure what to say. "I thought I was a couple of times, but not in a long time. You?"

She ignored his question. "Were you in love as an adult? Or are you talking about a 'music camp Joey'?"

"Good question. More music camp Joey. I think I was eighteen or nineteen the last time I thought I was in love." Until today.

"What happened?"

"Nothing happened. Summer romance. She went away to college, I was in the Navy, so time and distance..."

"What is it with girls leaving you for college? First Julie Baker and now this person."

He laughed. "Julie Baker. I can't believe you remembered her name?"

Her legs floated up from under her until her toes breached the water. "What was the other girl's name?"

"Connie Covington." He grinned. "I haven't thought of Connie in years."

"Was she pretty?"

"Yep. Long, blond hair that hit mid-back. Blue eyes. Rock'n body. Why?"

"She sounds beautiful."

He floated closer. "Not at beautiful as you, Ana. She couldn't hold a candle to you."

Her head dipped along with her gaze. "You don't have to say that."

He put two fingers under her chin and lifted until their gazes met. "You're right. I don't have to say it, but it's true. Has no one ever told you how beautiful you are? Can't you see your beauty in the mirror? Hell, Ana. The first time I laid eyes on you, I almost tripped over my own feet."

She gave him a shy smile. "When you were changing my tire?"

With a chuckle, he said, "Hon, you barely rolled the window down. All I saw were a pair of frantic eyes."

"I wasn't frantic," she said with a sniff.

"Scared?"

She grinned. "Maybe. I was in the middle of nowhere, driving a car I knew nothing about, and my rescuer looked like a badass on a motorcycle."

He laughed. "I loved that you tried to give me twenty bucks."

She dropped her head back into the water. "I was taught to pay people who help you."

He pulled her to him and kissed her thoroughly. "There. I'm paid in full."

"Well, gosh, you should've told me that last Friday."

He chuckled. "Oh, my lord. Can you imagine what you would've said?" Then he laughed loudly.

She joined him laughing.

"Hey," she said. "Another question. Have you ever skinny-dipped?"

He nodded. "Sure. Lots of times growing up, and probably more as a SEAL. Have you?"

She shook her head.

He waggled his eyebrows. "Want to?"

Her cheeks flushed. "Yeah, but..."

"Ah. Gotcha." He swam over to the ladder and climbed on the boat. "Have at it."

"You won't look?"

"Of course, I'm going to look. What if you drown? I'd feel horrible."

She laughed, and then sobered. "Okay. Here goes." She sunk below the swim noodle and came up behind it. She went under again and came up with her top in her hands. She hooked her arms over the noodle, leaving her body below the water.

He arched a brow. "How does that feel?"

"Freeing." Her smile was as bright as was the light in her eyes.

He held out his hand and wiggled his fingers. "C'mon. Let's have those bottoms."

She giggled and blushed. Then, in a rush of activity, she jerked them off and tossed both pieces up on the boat deck. She pushed away a little farther from the boat, which did nothing to cover what he could see through the crystal-clear water. Her carpet definitely matched the drapes.

"So? How does it feel?'

"Odd. I thought I'd feel like I was in a big bath, but it's nothing like that at all. It's hard to describe. The waves sort of tickle."

He grinned. "Oh yeah? Where?"

Her cheeks flamed. "Ha."

He'd turned his back when she said, "My mother is pressuring me to marry my manager's son."

His heart stopped as did the forward step he began to take. He lowered his foot back to the deck. "Oh. Are you going to?" He didn't turn around. He thought maybe she'd tell him more if she wasn't looking into his devastated expression.

He heard her sigh. "I don't want to. Geoffrey has been talking about marriage for a while. He asked me to marry him a couple of weeks ago."

"And you said...?" he asked, his voice rasping a bit.

"I said no, of course, but that didn't stop him from getting his father and my mother in on the persuasion." She sighed again. "When you saw me yesterday coming out of the office, I'd been checking my emails. Lots of rage from Randall from having to cancel this week's performances, but there was also an email from

Geoffrey, telling me that my mother was thrilled about us marrying, and she'd even reserved a venue for the wedding."

"I don't see the problem. Just tell him no. Tell your mom the same thing."

"You don't understand."

He turned to face her. "Then explain it in a way I can understand."

She floated a little closer to the boat. "My mother doesn't take no for an answer, even from my father. When I called home last night using your phone, I discovered she was out shopping for a wedding dress for me. I can almost guarantee she'll have the dress, location, date, and invitations ready to be mailed within the next ten days." She sighed. "I'll tell her no, but she won't listen. Geoffrey is poised to take over as my manager when Randall retires. Randall is almost sixty-five, so that could be any time."

He sat in the open door of the railing and rested his feet on the ladder. "How old is Geoffrey?"

"Ten years older than me, so, fortyish."

"Are you in love with him?"

"Oh, no. I mean, I've known him all my life. We're friends, but nothing else."

"So, he's not someone you've slept with?" He raised his hand to stop her from answering. "I only ask because maybe he's harboring feelings for you and thinks you are likewise."

"First, *eww*, gross," she said, grimacing. "I've never even kissed him, other than on the cheek at Christmas or New Year's Eve. And second, I'm pretty sure he's either bisexual or gay. As far as I know, he's never had a steady girl—or boy—friend."

"Ah. You're thinking he wants you as his beard."

She nodded. "And I think he'd love to tap my money."

He frowned. "Hello? You're gorgeous as fuck. Maybe that's why he wants you."

"I love that you think I'm attractive, but I honestly don't think he sees me the same way."

"And his dad is all in favor of this marriage?"

"Oh, yeah. Randall can retire and know he's leaving me in his son's hands."

"What about Geoffrey's mother? What does she say?"

Her face softened. "His mom died when Geoffrey was less than a year old. It's always been his father and him."

"There's so much wrong with this picture. I can see why you ran away."

"Yeah, the concerto, the pressure from Geoffrey…, it was all too much." She gave a sad chuckle. "The only way I can convince everyone that I'll never marry Geoffrey is to marry someone else and use my husband as the excuse, since, you know, the law frowns on more than one spouse."

"Okay. Let's get married," Sawyer blurted.

CHAPTER 11

Ana's head jerked back. "What?"

"I said, let's get married." When she gaped at him, he said, "Look, it'll buy you some time. As soon as this week is over, I'm being deployed. I can't say where and I don't know how long I'll be gone, but a husband, even one who isn't in the country, should be enough to stop you from being pressured into something you don't want. And," he hurried on to add, "this isn't pressure. I'm just offering you an alternative.

His heart shook as he spoke. He hadn't thought this out at all. His mouth had been fully engaged before his brain. Marrying Ana hadn't been front and center in his head, but maybe it'd been way back in the recesses, in his subconscious hiding, ready to jump out and surprise him—and her—without warning. But now that it was out there, the idea—which should have terrified him—didn't. He was all nerves about her answer. He'd live if she said no, but he'd die if she laughed.

But she wasn't laughing. She was studying him. Her face wore an expression of confusion and questioning. No smile. No twinkle in her eye. She was thinking.

Involuntarily, he held his breath.

"Yes," she said. "I will marry you."

He dropped heavily into the captain's chair. "I'm serious about this, Ana."

"I am, too. I like you, Sawyer. I like you a lot. You make me laugh. You make me happy. Two things I haven't experienced in a while. And I trust you. I know we haven't known each other long, but I feel like I can tell you anything, and you won't judge me. There's something about being with you that makes me feel stronger." She sighed and her face flushed. "And I'll admit, you're the best kisser I've ever kissed."

He grinned. "Is that so?"

She nodded. "But you need to know something."

He didn't respond, just gave her time to collect her thoughts.

"I'm not, well…" She scrunched her nose. "I'm not good at the whole sex thing."

His breath caught. "Not good? Or do you not want to have sex with me, because hon, I definitely want to have sex with you."

"Oh, I don't mind having sex. I mean…" She shrugged. "It's okay, I guess. I mean, sure, we can have sex. I don't want you to get your hopes up with me."

He bit the inside of his cheek to keep from laughing. "Ana, have you ever had an orgasm?"

She waved off his question. "That only happens in romance books for women."

His eyes closed as he fought a chuckle. "No, hon, women have orgasms."

"Really? I…."

"You never have. Well, I'll have to see what I can do about that."

"No, no. That's not what I mean. I'm probably frigid or something. I'm warning you so you aren't disappointed in me."

"You've never disappointed me, even when you wouldn't do the zipline on Sunday."

She chuckled. "This may be scarier than a zipline."

"True. Do you want to get married in California?"

She shrugged. "Let's go to Vegas. I haven't been there since I played with the Las Vegas Philharmonic two years ago."

"Vegas, huh?" He scratched his beard. "Okay. I'll need to get a haircut and shave."

"Seriously?"

"Well, yeah. I'm going to marry a famous concert pianist. I need to look like I deserve to."

She smiled. "I really like you, Sawyer."

"Good. I really like you too, Ana. We might need to cut our day short if we're going to do this."

"Tomorrow is my birthday," she said, as though he'd forgotten. "I want to get married on my birthday."

"Okay. I can do that. I need to reach out to a friend. I think I can get us speedier transportation than my Harley or Barbie."

She paddled to the boat. "Can I handle the hotel and wedding arrangements?"

"Of course." He looked down at her naked body and got immediately aroused. "I assume you want to wait until after the wedding to sleep together? I mean, if not, I'm game to head back to the cabin right now."

"I want to wait." She gave him a sad smile. "Once

you're married to me, how awful I am in bed can't scare you off."

"Oh, hon. You can't scare me off."

"Can I have my swimsuit back?"

"I don't know," he said with a grin. "I need to see what I'm getting."

"Sawyer. You think I don't know you've been ogling me this whole time?" She lifted her hand and let water run through her fingers. "This water is crystal clear."

He gave her a guilty grin. "You caught me."

She rolled her eyes, and wiggled her fingers. "Please."

He dropped the bottoms into her outstretched hand. She slipped them on and waited. When he playfully arched a brow, she sighed, tossed her float noodle through the open railing door, and climbed up the ladder. His heart almost stopped. Her breasts were perfect...full and round. Her nipples were rosy pink and erect.

"Look your fill," she said.

"I plan to." He caught her around her waist and pull her against him. Her breasts mashed into his chest. Nothing had ever felt that good. "Kiss me, Future Mrs. Beckett."

She grinned and kissed him, her mouth open, her tongue seeking his.

He felt her heart pound against his chest. When he pulled his mouth back, she whimpered her protest.

"Let's head back." His voice was gruff.

"Let's stay here and make-out," she replied and kissed him again, this time rubbing her nipples through his chest hair.

He growled and pulled her firmer against him. "Keep this up and the wedding night will be tonight. We could get married right now. No need to go to Vegas. There's no wait for a license in California."

"I know this will sound crazy, but there's something about a Vegas wedding."

He leaned back until their gazes held. "And, if I'm understanding your mother, will it be the perfect 'fuck you' to your mother?"

"It would, yes, but I love Vegas. The lights. All the stars there. Marriage is a gamble, especially the way we're doing it, so let's do it there."

"You're crazy," he said and leaned toward her to kiss her. "Luckily for you, I love crazy."

They returned the boat and headed back to Harbin's Harbor Cabins.

"Okay, I'm going to call my favorite hotel and book a room for us. Then I'll find out about getting married tomorrow," she said as they walked the trail to their cabins.

"Yeah, I've got a couple of calls to make. I'll come back when I have my end lined up."

WHEN SHE'D PACKED TO RUN AWAY, AVA HAD MOSTLY packed casual clothes. She'd had no idea how long she'd be gone. However, she'd stuffed a couple of her long performance gowns in Barbie's trunk. She had no idea why she'd done that, but they were a couple of her favorites, and she couldn't leave them behind.

Now, it seemed like those would come in handy.

It was close to five when Sawyer knocked on her

door. Her heart jumped and bumped around in her chest. She was marrying that cute boy from Germany! This marriage was crazy, but most of her life had been nutso. This was just another piece in her life puzzle.

"Come in," she called from the living room where she sat making a list of what she needed to get done.

"Hi," he said, almost shyly. "Have you come to your senses and changed your mind?"

She laughed. "Not only have I *not* changed my mind, I'm excited. I got the hotel reserved, and the concierge was so helpful with the wedding plans." She grinned. "I realized I could change the password on my credit card account so that Randall can't see my charges. I don't know why I hadn't thought about that before now. What about you? Change your mind?"

"Oh, hell no. I am so marrying up."

She laughed. "You say that now, but you haven't met my family."

He walked over to where she sat on the sofa, lowered himself to the cushion, and pulled her in for a hug. "I'm a SEAL. I've faced all kinds of bad people. Your family doesn't scare me."

Again, she laughed. "My grandparents could get Al-Qaeda on the run."

"Perfect. We could use them in the military."

She wrinkled her nose. "Want to hear the plans?"

"Sure." He settled against the sofa back. "Then I'll tell you mine."

"Okay. We have a room at a hotel I want to surprise you with, but you'll like it. I promise. We can fill out the marriage license application online today. It'll be quicker. Now you tell me yours."

"I have a friend whose family owns an aviation

company. He's flying a plane up to us here this evening so I can us fly to Vegas."

"You're kidding."

Sawyer shook his head. "Nope. His name is Paul Grotto. He was a SEAL until he left a couple of years ago to join the family business. He owes me a favor or two."

"I didn't know you could fly a plane."

"And a helicopter, if need be." He shrugged. "Man's gotta have hobbies."

She laughed and snuggled into his side. "I wish we didn't have to wait until tomorrow."

"Hey, that's what you wanted. I was ready the second you agreed."

She sat up and looked at him. "He's coming tonight?"

"Yeah. Dropping off the plane and taking my Harley back. I'll fly the plane back to him when I leave. Why?"

"Well, this is a crazy idea, but let's still get married on the ninth, but we can do it at midnight tonight. That'd be tomorrow officially."

He smiled. "Pack up, Future Mrs. Beckett. Let's do that."

Since Sawyer's friend was scheduled to fly up after the end of the work day, they had a little time to kill. Ana insisted they go ahead and fill out the marriage license form, which they did. Since neither had ever been married, and both were over the age of consent, it was an easy application.

Then Ana telephoned Caesar's Palace to see if the Marc & Cleopatra suite was available for the next two nights. She smiled when she discovered it was, and now it was theirs. That suite was so over the top, she was sure it would blow Sawyer away.

The call from Sawyer's friend came at close to eight. He was ten minutes out from the Lake Kincade airport, and he had a surprise with him. Sawyer rode his bike while Ana followed in Barbie since Paul intended on taking Sawyer's bike back to San Diego.

Lake Kincade was small with only one landing strip, so finding Paul and his plane presented no challenge. A white and tan Cessna taxied to a stop. An attendant approached the plane, placing airplane chocks at the wheels. The door opened and a petite blonde with the figure of a Vegas showgirl hurried down the stairs and over to where Sawyer stood with Ana.

"Sawyer Beckett." The woman raced across the tarmac and threw her arms around his neck.

Sawyer laughed and picked the woman up his arms. Then, to Ana's shock, the woman kissed Sawyer on the lips!

"Hey," a deep voice shout. "Get your hands off my wife if you know what's good for you."

Sawyer turned toward the large man stalking toward them. Ana would've run if she'd faced this man in a dark alley. He looked terrifying.

Instead, Sawyer released the woman and grasped the extended hand of the man.

"Paul. Thank you, man. I can't believe Patty came."

"I tried to leave her home, but you know Patty."

The petite woman wrapped her arm around Paul's waist. "When Paul told me what you were up to, do not believe for one second I wasn't coming along to see the lucky woman who'd gotten you on your knees." She looked at Ana. "I'm Patty Grotto, Paul's wife." Her eyes narrowed and after a long pause, she said, "You're Ana Cristiano, right?"

Ana's mouth dropped. No one recognized her outside of a concert hall. "I am. Have we met?"

Patty shook her head. "I'm a fan."

"You're kidding," Ana said.

"I'm not. I am a classical music fanatic." She tilted her head toward Paul. "This is Paul, my husband, who only listens to hard rock." She leaned forward. "Gives me a headache."

Paul held out his hand to Ana. "I'm Paul. I'm thrilled to meet you. Sawyer couldn't stop talking about you on the phone. That's why we're little late. I had to get some work done, and he wouldn't let me off the phone."

Ana was suddenly engulfed in Sawyer's arms.

"What can I say? I took one look and knew she was the one."

"Well, I for one, am so excited," Patty said.

Sawyer frowned. "Are you riding on the Harley back to San Diego with Paul?"

"No, silly," Patty said. "As soon as Paul told me what was happening, I packed our bags. We're coming with you. You're going to need witnesses."

And that was how Ana found herself in a seat next to a chatty woman she'd just met, while her future husband sat in the co-pilot's seat next to Paul.

Patty grabbed Ana's hand. "I am so excited…probably more than I was the day I got married."

"You've known Sawyer long?"

"Gosh, at least ten years. He's adorable, right? Well, of course, right. You're marrying him, so obviously you think he's adorable." Patty squeezed Ana's hand. "You're a lucky, lucky woman. Now, I understand and forgive you cancelling your concerts this week."

Ana's eyes opened wide. "You had tickets to my concerto?"

"Yep. My sister and me. Our husbands are music heathens." Patty laughed. "She'll die when she finds out I got to go to your wedding instead." Patty's face got serious. "That's okay, isn't it? I didn't even ask. If you don't want us there, that's fine, too. It was a good excuse to leave our kids with my folks and get away for a spontaneous vacation. But say the word, and Paul and I will disappear."

Ana smiled. She liked this friend of Sawyer's. Over the years, Ana hadn't had many, or really any, good female friends. Gosh, or male friends either, now that she thought about it. Her life had been piano, Randall, Geoffrey, and travel. Patty would make an excellent maid of honor.

"Of course, I want you there. I need a maid of honor…if you want to do it."

Patty hugged her. "I'd love it. Are you sure you have to marry tonight? We could do a last-minute bachelorette party. Hit all the bars." Her eyebrows waggled. "Pick up some men."

Sawyer turned in his seat. "Did I hear you encouraging the woman who's going to be my wife to go to bars and hit on men?"

He fake-glared at her, which made Patty laugh. He looked pretty fierce to Ana, but she, like Patty, knew him well enough now to recognize his kidding.

"I want her to know she has choices," Patty said, with a snort.

"No, she doesn't," Sawyer replied. "I got her to agree to marry me, Patty. I want to keep it that way."

"*Ohh*, so caveman," Patty said.

"That's okay, Patty. I know what's out there for me, and I pick Sawyer." Ana smiled at him. "He's kind of perfect."

"Yeah, I can see that," Patty replied.

Ana glanced out of the window. "How far out are we? I'm supposed to let the hotel know our expected arrival time so they can send a car."

Sawyer spoke with Paul and then turned to Ana. "About twenty minutes." He pulled his phone from his pants pocket and handed it to her. "You can call now, as long as you have a signal."

There was a strong signal. She dialed.

"Good evening. Caesar's Palace."

"Hello. This is Ana Cristiano. I have a reservation for this evening. I need the car to pick us up at the airport."

"Hold please."

Music played as she waited. Then, "Good evening, Ms. Cristiano. This is Charles, your personal concierge. Everything is ready for your arrival and wedding. Is there anything else I need to do for you other than send the limo?"

"Yes, please. There is another couple with us. They will need a room."

"Yes, ma'am. Another suite, then?"

"Yes."

"On your tab, or will they be starting their own?"

"Mine, of course."

"Yes, ma'am."

"Yes. Did you make an appointment at the marriage license bureau for this evening?"

"The car will take you directly to the Clark County Clerk's office. There might be a slight wait if someone is already being served, but you will go to the front of the line. Anything else?"

"No. That's all. Send the car now."

"Yes, ma'am. It will be waiting."

She clicked off and handed the phone to Sawyer. "We are set and ready to go." She wondered what Sawyer had brought in the way of clothing. It didn't matter. This wedding would happen even if he wore shorts.

They landed and parked. As soon as they stopped moving, a red carpet was rolled out to the plane's door. Patty was the first one off, followed by Ana, Sawyer, and finally Paul.

"Make sure the plane is gassed up and ready to go on…," Ana looked at Sawyer. "Friday? Or Saturday?"

Sawyer looked at Paul for the answer. But it was Patty who said, "Saturday. I want to drag this out as long as I can."

Ana chuckled. "Saturday, then."

"Yes, ma'am."

A silver Rolls Royce stood on the tarmac. A uniformed chauffer stood beside an open rear door.

"That's our ride," Ana said. Sawyer was looking at her like she'd grown two heads on the flight. "What?"

"I've just never seen you like this."

She chuckled. "You're in my world now, darling. This is my comfort zone."

He put his arm around her. "Apparently."

While they were loading into the back of the Rolls, their luggage was transferred from the plane to the car's trunk. The chauffer slid into the front seat and clicked an intercom button.

"Good evening. I'm Samuel. There's champagne and strawberries to enjoy on your trip. I should have you at the marriage bureau in about fifteen minutes. If you need anything, please don't hesitate to press the intercom. I'll raise the glass for your privacy. And let me be the first to welcome you to Las Vegas and congratulate the happy couple."

Happy couple. The words rang in Ana's ears. Sure, she was happy. She was getting everything she wanted in the marriage, but what was Sawyer getting? A woman who didn't like sex. At least she'd gotten the Marc & Cleopatra Suite as a surprise. She hoped he enjoyed it, and besides, it wasn't as if she couldn't afford it. At a little under twenty-thousand a night, she had enough money to practically live there if she wanted. Still, it had a piano, and for the first time in a very long time, she wanted to play…for him.

The stop at the marriage bureau was quick, and then they were back in the Rolls heading to their suite in under ten minutes. Filling out the forms online had expedited the process tremendously.

Back inside the car, Patty refilled champagne glasses for the return trip. "To your long life and happiness."

"Agreed," her husband said. "Congratulations, you two."

Ana's face heated. Paul and Patty didn't know this was a sham marriage designed to get her out of another one. She thought about telling them, but then, Sawyer said, "Thank you. I adore this woman. I am the happiest man who ever lived."

The four clinked glasses and drank. Well, she wasn't going to be the one to spill the beans if he wasn't.

"What about rings?" Patty asked.

"I've got that handled," Ana said.

"You do?" Sawyer asked with surprised expression.

"You agreed to let me handle all the arrangements, so yeah. It's handled. Trust me."

He hugged her. "I trust you."

And she realized how much she trusted him. And just like that, any reservation she might have harbored about this quickie wedding evaporated.

CHAPTER 12

The Rolls pulled up at a private door at the rear of Caesar's Palace.

"What's this?" Patty asked.

"Private entrance," Ana explained. "We have a private elevator to our suite, which will probably take you to your room also."

"Sweet," Patty said with a grin. She looked at her husband. "This is how the other half lives."

Ana laughed. "No, nothing like that. I've played here a couple of times and the hotel management knows me. That's all."

She wasn't exactly lying. She had performed a concerto here, and the hotel staff did know her, but with her family money, this *was* how the other half, or rather, the upper one-percent lived. But no one needed to know that.

The luggage was unloaded, and Charles met them at the elevator. "Good evening, Ms. Cristiano, Mr. Beckett. Everything is ready for your arrival. I have your guests in the Octavius Suite. I hope that's acceptable."

"It's perfect. Thank you."

"If you'll follow me."

Patty and Paul were led away to a different elevator. Ana and Sawyer rode with Charles to the top for their penthouse suite. When they entered, Sawyer's eyes popped wide.

"Holy shit, Ana."

"Yeah," she said with a smile. "I love this room."

Charles directed the porters with the luggage to the main bedroom. Dining services followed with a cart.

"I took the liberty of ordering a light dinner," Charles said. "After we spoke today, I feared you might miss dinner."

"Thank you," Ana said. "I have to keep my groom happy."

"Your groom is too stunned to speak," Sawyer said.

Charles checked his watch. "The jeweler will be here momentarily with your ring selections."

Sawyer looked at her, his eyebrows raised.

She shrugged. "I didn't have time to ask what kind of ring you wanted, so the jeweler is bringing a selection. I told him to focus on titanium since it's the most durable. I wasn't sure if you would wear it..." she paused, "at work." She wasn't sure if SEALs wore wedding rings, but she wanted him to have a memento of their marriage.

"And your ring?" he asked. "Do I get to pick that out?"

She grinned. "Yep. There will be a selection of those." She leaned closer so Charles wouldn't overhear. "But I'll be paying for it, and don't argue. I think I know what I want, and I don't expect you to have to pay for all of this. You're doing me the favor."

"Oh, honey, this isn't a favor. Trust me. I want to be here, doing this."

"I know," she said, "but without Randall and my mother's antics, we'd be going our separate ways this weekend." She saddened at that realization. It was true, and she'd have been extremely forlorn driving back to San Diego. Now, she got to take him with her, if only in her heart.

Over a light dinner of crab cakes, waffle fries, and drinks—bourbon for him and Diet Coke for her—they met with the jeweler.

Sawyer looked over the variety of groom's rings. She immediately saw her favorite for him. There were some beautiful rings in black, or silver, or gold, but there was something about the black titanium that seemed like Sawyer.

He pointed to the black titanium. "That one."

A bright smile stretched her mouth. "That's exactly the one I had in mind, too."

"Great minds," he said and kissed her. "Now, what do you have for my bride?"

"Some excellent rings for her to pick from." The jeweler set the groom's rings back into his case and pulled out two trays of diamond rings.

Sawyer's face paled as he studied the rings. Ana placed her hand over his as reassurance. These were all a little too gaudy for her tastes. Plus, Sawyer looked like he was going to pass out.

"These are all lovely," she said, "but I'm afraid, with my job, they're all a little too top heavy with those large stones. I wouldn't be able to wear them when I play. Do you have anything not so large?"

"I do, but are you sure none of these are to your liking?"

For years, Ana had watched her mother deal with pushy salespeople who wanted to sell the most expensive item to her, even if that wasn't what she'd asked for. Ana couldn't blame the salesperson. Their job was to sell and make a commission.

"I'm sure. What else do you have?"

With a long-suffering sigh that almost made Ana laugh, the salesman replaced the two trays and brought out a third. Although more compact and smaller stones, these rings were still stunningly gorgeous. Ana studied the rings, removing one and then another.

"Do you see one you like?" she asked Sawyer.

"There are a couple I like more than others, but this is your ring. You're the one who'll be wearing it. Pick out whichever makes you happy."

She smiled up at him. "You make me happy. No ring will ever bring me as much joy as you do."

The jeweler seemed to love her reply because he beamed at her.

Ana picked up a ring to study it. "Tell me about this one, please."

"An excellent choice. The center stone is a five-point-nine caret grade F, colorless stone with no imperfections. The shape is called radiant. It's flanked on both sides by baguette-cut diamonds, also colorless. The two bands surrounding the main one contain thirty-six, round-cut diamonds in grade G, for a total caret weight of four. The caret weight for the set is nine-point-nine."

"This is the one," she said and looked at Sawyer, who smiled. "This one?"

"Exactly the one I had my eye on."

"Perfect. I'd like to try this one, but I'd rather my groom not see it on my finger until he puts it there."

Sawyer stood. "Say no more. I'll, um, step outside on the terrace."

As soon as he was out of the room, Ana slipped the ring on. It fit but was a little loose. "I'll need this adjusted tomorrow. Have Sawyer try his ring on and you'll adjust it tomorrow, if necessary."

"Yes, ma'am."

"You've spoken with Caesar's about payment?"

"I have. Are you sure you don't want to look at either of those first two trays? A woman with your discriminating taste might enjoy a more, let's say, eye-catching ring."

What he didn't say was a woman with your disposable funds.

"No. This is exactly what I want. Thank you for coming out so late and bringing such an outstanding selection." She smiled. "You made it tough to decide."

"My pleasure. I'll check with Charles tomorrow about resizing. I'll step outside with your groom and check the ring."

The doorbell rang, and Charles opened the suite's door to admit Paul and Patty. Their shorts and T-shirts had been replaced with a black suit for Paul and a floor-length black gown for Patty.

"Wow," Ana said. "You two clean up pretty good."

Patty laughed and whirled in a circle. "Isn't it lovely? I've only gotten to wear it once, and this seemed like a great excuse to pull it out of my closet." Her brow pulled into a frown. "Have you looked at the time? You need to get dressed."

"I know. Paul, Sawyer is on the terrace if you'd like

to join him. Help yourself to a drink. There are some munchies on the table if you're hungry."

Paul saluted and walked outside to where Sawyer stood with the jeweler.

The doorbell rang again, and Charles admitted two women carrying black cases.

"Hair and make-up," Ana said to Patty. "This way." She led Patty and the two women to a second bedroom where her dress awaited.

"Piano concertos must pay better than I thought," Patty muttered.

Ana chuckled. "You have no idea."

SAWYER WAS DRESSED AND READY TO GET THIS SHOW ON the road. Paul had brought Sawyer's dress blues from his closet in his motorhome, which is really why it had taken him until almost eight to get to Lake Kincade. Sawyer figured he would only marry once in his life. When this was over with Ana, and he was sure Ana would leave him within the year when she didn't need his protection any longer, he wouldn't need these blues for a wedding, unless he was a groomsman for someone else. He never intended to marry again. He was a one-woman man, and Ana was that woman for him. She'd never believe him if he told her that. Hell, he'd fallen the minute he'd seen her with Ranger Saturday morning. It was as if his heart had said, "This one. This is who you've been waiting for." Of course, he'd never tell anyone that. They would think he was nuts, but he wasn't crazy, except crazy about the woman he was about to marry.

He stood on the terrace alongside the private

infinity pool. Pots of blooming flowers sat around the edge and on the tables. The flames from tiki torches flickered in the light breeze. A full moon shone overhead, lighting the area, so the torches provided more ambiance than necessary light.

The woman who was performing the ceremony arrived ten minutes before midnight. She told him her name was Amanda Larson, and she'd performed hundreds of these ceremonies. Caesar's general manager was a personal friend of hers and had asked her to do this wedding as a favor.

"I appreciate your doing this then," Sawyer said. "I know it was last minute."

Amanda waved him off. "Happy to do it. The timing is perfect. I just finished a wedding in the chapel, so I was going to be onsite anyway. Now, do you have any special requests in the vows?"

"I'd like to say something to Ana when you've gone through the traditional vows."

"No problem. Now, if you'll excuse me, I'd like to speak with your bride."

Amanda disappeared into the bedroom Ana had commandeered.

Paul handed Sawyer a glass of bourbon neat and then tapped it with his glass. "I'm happy for you, man. Good luck."

"Listen, I'm deploying soon. Can you and Patty stay in touch with Ana and make sure she's okay?"

"Of course. Deployment. That sucks. No wonder you wanted to do this before you left. What about the military paperwork of adding a wife?"

"I've notified my team leader and commanding officer. Both assured me they'd take care of it."

"Nervous?"

"Nope."

Paul laughed. "I was shaking like a leaf in a hurricane the day I married Patty."

"Okay, I lied. I'm scared to death she'll realize before the wedding that she can do so much better."

Paul slapped him on the back. "I know the feeling, but your lady looks at you like you hold all the secrets to life. I don't think she's going to back out."

Sawyer took a gulp of bourbon, enjoying the burn as it rolled down his throat. "I hope you're right."

Somewhere, a clock struck midnight. Amanda exited the bedroom and walked to where the men stood.

"It's a beautiful night for a wedding. It's time to get started."

Charles started a recording of Mendelssohn's "Wedding March." Sawyer wouldn't have known the composer if he hadn't looked it up. He'd wondered whether Ana would choose it, and was happy that she had. It felt like a wedding.

The bedroom door opened, and Patty walked out carrying a single long-stemmed red rose. She walked across the living room and outside. She stopped and kissed Sawyer's cheek before moving to stand at the side.

Then his bride walked out. His knees almost gave way. She wore a white off-the shoulder gown that clung to her figure. The material at the shoulders appeared to cross over her breasts and disappear into the dress, which nipped in at her waist, and then flared at her hips. As she walked toward him, a long slit on the right side flashed her thigh.

Her hair was flowing down her back, exactly as he loved it. Her face glowed with the smile on her mouth.

She carried six, long-stemmed, red roses tied with a white ribbon that trailed in curls down the front of her dress.

She neared him, and he swallowed the lump in his throat. His only regret was not having his parents here, but somewhere, he'd seen a video photographer capturing the wedding. They would enjoy that.

"Hey," she said with a whisper as she stepped beside him. "You look incredible. You shaved and cut your hair."

"Honey, I don't hold a candle to you."

Amanda cleared her throat and began. After both Ana and Sawyer went through their vows, Amanda said, "Sawyer would like to say something, I believe…?"

Sawyer nodded. He looked into Ana's glistening eyes. "I know how lucky I am to have you in my life. I promise I will hold you in my heart until my dying days."

A tear ran down Ana's face. "Darn you," she whispered. "You messed up my makeup."

He used his gloved thumb to dab away her tear. "I meant every word. I want you to know that."

"I do. I am lucky to have you. I trust you. I adore you. I love you. You will be in my heart forever."

"Oh, babe, I love you, too."

They stared into each other's eyes until Amanda said, "By the power invested in me by the state of Nevada, I pronounce you husband and wife. You can kiss your bride, Mr. Beckett."

Patty and Paul cheered as Sawyer dipped Ana into a kiss.

There was cake, of course. Ana, or maybe it was Charles, hadn't forgotten a thing. Cake and champagne were consumed on the terrace with Ana sitting on his lap.

"Play for me," Sawyer said.

"Okay. Anything?"

"Anything."

The four adults walked to the grand piano in the living room, the photographer changing from the still camera around his neck to the video camera he'd left on the floor when he'd thought he was done.

Ana sat. Sawyer stood on her right side, while Paul and Patty took the left. She sat there for a minute and began to play. The piece started slow, with dramatic strikes on the keys. The music was at first heavy, almost sad, but then her fingers began to fly over the keys. He could barely keep up with her hands. The music became fast and happy. He could feel her emotions in the notes. The piece ended, but it hadn't been nearly long enough for him.

"What was that?" he asked.

"I know," Patty shouted.

"You do not," her husband said. "And that's our cue for leaving. By the way, Ana, I don't know who you talked to about getting us a room, but it's a fucking suite."

"Don't say fucking," Patty slurred out. "We don't want them to know what we're going to be doing next."

Ana laughed as did Sawyer.

"It'll be our secret," Ana assured her.

Patty shushed with a finger to her mouth. "And your fucking secret is safe with us."

Ana frowned and looked at Sawyer. "She's drunk," he whispered. "I think she means our fucking tonight, not anything else. They don't know anything else."

She nodded, but he saw the flash in her eyes.

They left, the photographer following them out the door.

"Finally," Sawyer said. "I thought they'd never leave."

Ana chuckled.

"I love the way you play. So dramatic and your fingers…wow. They flew."

"Thank you," she rising and taking a bow. "That was the third concerto by Rachmaninoff."

"That was incredible. Thank you."

"Anything for you, Sawyer."

He gave her a leer. "Anything?"

ANA STOOD IN FRONT OF THE MIRRORED WARDROBE doors with Sawyer standing behind her. After swooping her up into his arms to walk with her to the bedroom, he'd set her on her feet in front of the mirrors and told her not to move.

Methodically, he undressed himself, taking time to hang up his dress trousers and jacket, placing his shoes in the closet on the floor, folding his white button-down shirt, even his T-shirt and boxers, before he turned to her.

By then, she was trembling, nearly salivating. This Sawyer, so contained, his expression almost remote, had her nipples hardening, her thighs clenching.

The smoky look in his eyes as strode toward her had her biting her lip to suppress a moan. Although she was still doubtful he'd be able to wring an orgasm from her, there was pleasure in just looking at him.

When he stood beside her, he raised her left hand

and kissed the backs of her fingers. The diamonds in her rings glittered, shocking her a bit. She'd really done this. She'd really said her vows and let him slide the bands onto her finger. She was a married woman, and this well-built warrior was her husband.

He knelt and patted his thigh.

She lifted one foot and then the other and let him slide her shoes from her feet. Each time, he did so, he kissed the top of her foot before placing it on the floor. When he stood again, he moved behind her and went about opening her dress and sliding it upwards. Without being told what to do, she raised her arms.

Standing now in only her underwear and hose, she waited as he rolled down her thigh high stockings, his rough palms smoothing up her legs once they were bared. She couldn't contain a quiver when he neared the apex of her thighs, and she noted how much darker his eyes appeared as he bent toward her and pressed a kiss through the scrap of satin covering her sex.

Again, he straightened and moved behind her, his gaze locking with hers in the mirror as he unclipped her bra and drew it off her arms.

Then his hands cupped her breasts, his thumbs scraping the tips. She leaned back against his chest and watched as he caressed her soft flesh and bent to kiss the top of one shoulder.

"You are so beautiful, Ana."

"Thank you," she breathed, not really knowing how to answer.

When he scooped her up again, she gave a little cry. He walked the few steps to the large bed covered in a satin duvet, the corners folded down by the staff. When he bent over the bed, she reached out and grabbed the corner and tossed it back so he could set her in the center of the bed, one knee on the mattress as he deposited her and slowly slid his hands from underneath her.

When he reached into the drawer of the night stand, she encircled his wrist and shook her head.

"You're sure?" he asked.

She was sure she hoped for consequences, and she didn't want anything between them, not even a thin cloak of latex. In answer, she simply held out her arms.

Sawyer climbed fully onto the bed and over her body, resting on his elbows while his cock fell against her mound, so heavy and warm, her inner channel clenched again. She was wet. Ready for him to take her. Eager to see whether it was possible she might come with the right man.

He cupped the sides of her face and feathered a thumb across her bottom lip. "I meant what I said..."

She smiled. "I did, too. I love you."

Sawyer's nostrils flared and he bent to take her mouth. The kiss began sweetly, a soft rubbing of mouths, but as always seemed to happen with them, it very quickly grew heated.

She bit his lip and pulled, letting it go then giving him a challenging look.

His eyes narrowed and abruptly scooted downward, his mouth diving toward a breast. With one hand fondling the other breast, he sucked her nipple into his mouth and drew hard. Her toes curled, and then her knees rose to cup his sides. The pull of his mouth seemed to tug at something deep inside her belly, and she was instantly eager for him to take his attentions lower down her body.

However, Sawyer wasn't in any hurry. He plied

both breasts with nips of his teeth and sexy glides of his tongue. When he sucked at the tips, she couldn't help turning her head side to side and tightening around him. The pleasure was so intense, she realized she'd never felt anything approaching it, even full-on sex with her previous partners.

When he finally moved lower, she wasn't sure if she was disappointed, but she cupped her breasts to keep them warm and give herself comfort as he lightly bit and sucked at the skin of her belly, moving lower and lower until he rested between her legs, his head hovering above her sex.

She wasn't sure how she felt about that. It was disconcerting to say the least. Yes, she was aware that people had oral sex, but she wasn't sure if she was ready to leave herself so vulnerable to his gaze and touch. His gaze rose from her pussy to meet hers. Then he dipped downward, still looking at her, and trailed his tongue through her folds.

Her mouth opened on a gasp. The stroke was delightful, ending with a little pressure against the knot at the top of her folds. "Again," she gasped, her eyelids drifting downward.

Thankfully, Sawyer was amenable. As he used his fingers and tongue to stroke and penetrate her, her legs grew restless, her belly undulated, uncontrollably.

"Sawyer…" she whispered, gripping his hair to tug at him, needing him to come upward because she was about to explode.

"Let it happen, sweetheart," he said. Then he pressed two fingers inside her, thrusting them inward then pulling out, and latched his mouth around her hardening clitoris.

When his tongue flicked it, her back arched and she cried out, giving a strangled cry.

Moments later, he was cradling her face, kissing her mouth and cheeks. "God, you were so beautiful," he said, then pressed a hard kiss against her mouth.

When he pulled back, she blinked at him. "That was it, right? That…"

His mouth curved. "You had an orgasm. What do you think?"

She sighed, and her mouth slid into a happy smile. "I've never felt anything more wonderful. Can I do it again?"

SAWYER'S BODY ACHED TO JOIN WITH HERS, BUT HE'D never felt more satisfaction than he did at this moment. The look on her face when she'd crested made him feel like a conquering warrior. He'd have beat his chest in triumph if she hadn't needed him to hold her as she came back down.

Everything about the moment would be etched in his memory forever. Her pale dewy skin, her swollen lips rounding in surprise.

Her hands slid over his ass, and she dug her fingernails into his skin. "I mean it. I want to do that again."

Ready to oblige, he began to move downward again, but she gripped his ass harder. "You, inside me."

"Ah." And he grinned before coming up on his forearms, which exposed her body and his to both their gazes.

Her glance swept down his body. "Oh my. You look bigger from this angle."

"I'm the same amount of big, darling."

SAWYER AND ANA DIDN'T SEE PAUL AND PATTY AGAIN until dinner on Friday. And as soon as dinner was over, they left. Sawyer had to chuckle to himself. He and Ana could barely stop touching each other…a hand to a forearm, an arm around a waist, a kiss in her hair, or on her cheek. He was glad to see his friends, but even happier when they left.

Saturday morning, the four friends took the Rolls Royce to the airport for the flight back to Lake Kincade. When they touched down back in California, Sawyer lacked the words to thank his friends for their help.

The four of them stood on the tarmac.

"Listen," Sawyer sighed. "Thank you doesn't seem like enough."

"Man, say nothing," Paul said. "Patty and I haven't had this kind of time to ourselves since the twins were born. The suite was incredible, so thank you to both of you for that."

"I'll be lucky if baby number four doesn't arrive in nine months." Patty giggled. "I couldn't keep Paul out of my bath."

Paul rolled his eyes. "Best of luck, guys. Patty has your number, Ana?"

"Yes. I made sure of that."

"Then, I guess we'd better get home before our kids forget us."

Sawyer and Ana walked to their individual rides.

"See you at the cabin?" Sawyer said.

"I'll race you there, but wait—which cabin are we using?"

He laughed. "Yours is bigger than mine, so yours.

And we aren't racing. Barbie would be crushed by Harley."

She shook her head. "Oh, we'll see about that."

She slammed her car into reverse, spun around, and took off.

That woman would drive him crazy…and he looked forward to it for as long as he had her.

CHAPTER 13

S aturday night, they placed calls to their families via scheduled video chats.

His parents were surprised, but supportive. Of course, they were disappointed they hadn't been there, but relaxed when Sawyer explained there was a video of the entire wedding. His parents said they were heading back to the states soon and would reach out to her when they got back since Sawyer would be deployed.

When she'd asked him where he was being deployed, he had told her Africa but that was all he could say. To his parents, he just said deployment.

SEAL missions are classified and need-to-know. His parents were both aware of that. His dad accepted his deployment as any military personnel would. After being married to his father for so long, his mother was accustomed to mission secrecy, so neither parent asked any questions.

The call to her parents went pretty much as she'd

expected. Her mother went completely off the rails, not that Ana had expected anything less.

"But I already have your dress picked out and the venue reserved," her mother had cried. "Geoffrey will be crushed."

"I doubt it," Ana said, referring to Geoffrey, not her mother securing a venue. "Besides, you should have talked to me before making plans for *my* wedding."

"How?" her mother demanded. "You disappeared and wouldn't answer my calls."

"And that didn't suggest a problem? I wasn't ever going to marry Geoffrey, mom. That was your and Randall's dream, not mine. I'm sure Geoffrey will be disappointed, but he'll live. Besides..." She pulled Sawyer closer. "This is the man I'm married to."

Her mother lifted her nose in the air. "I can't believe you ran off and had a tacky Vegas wedding. How could you? Do you have any idea how that's going to play in Chicago society?"

Sawyer looked at her, a questioning expression on his face.

"I don't care about Chicago society," Ana said. "Only you and Grandmother Zeller care about that."

"Well, I'm sure it's easy to get a quickie Vegas marriage annulled," her mother said.

Ana scoffed. "Not happening."

"We'll see about that. I hope to God you had the sense to get a prenup."

This time when Sawyer looked at her, his eyebrows rose. "I'm sorry, what?"

"I did not. We didn't need one."

"Oh, you foolish girl. Of course, you need one. This...this...*man* could—"

"That's enough, Mother. This man, as you call him, has a name. Sawyer Beckett. He's an honorable man."

Her mother scoffed.

For the first time, her father spoke. "Congratulations, Kitten."

"Thank you, Daddy. I'm really happy." She looked at Sawyer, and then back at her dad. "He makes me laugh. I'm always first, and I trust him with my whole heart."

Her father beamed. "That's all I can ask for. Sawyer?"

"Yes, sir," Sawyer replied.

"You take good care of my baby."

"Yes, sir. Of course."

Her father's eyes narrowed. "I'm serious. Anything happens, or you hurt her in any way, your life is over. Got me?"

Ana gasped. She'd never heard her father threaten anyone. "Daddy!"

"It's not an idle threat," he said.

Sawyer's expression was solemn when he said, "You don't have to worry about me, sir. However, I do ask that her mother and her manager give her more breathing room. I won't have my wife harassed, even by people who think they know better. Ana is an adult and I expect to hear that she's being treated as such."

Her father smiled. "I agree, Sawyer." He looked at his wife. "Back off, Irene."

Her mother began to cry. "I only wanted what was best for her."

Her father nodded and handed a box of tissues to his wife. "You've got our word, Sawyer."

"Thank you."

They didn't call her manager because he was her

manager, not her family. Instead, Ana sent him a text explaining she'd gotten married and would be back in San Diego tomorrow. Additionally, she asked that he not call this evening.

Sunday morning was hell. She clung to Sawyer, tears rolling down her cheeks.

"It's not fair," she wailed. "I just find you, and the stupid Navy wants to send you away from me."

He smiled and kissed her. "Oh, honey. They can take me out of the country, but they can't take you out of my heart. You hear me?" He patted his chest. "You are here."

"And you are in my heart," she said with a cry. "Can we at least talk while you're gone?"

"Of course. I can call you, or text, even do computer chats. It might not be every day. That depends on what we're doing, but I'll try. I promise. I have only one request."

"Anything," she said with a sniff.

"Every time you play a concerto, I want to listen. I don't care if it's on the phone, or some computer link, but I love hearing you play. When you played for me after the wedding, well, it was something I'll never forget."

"I will. It'll be in every contract. I have to have a way to broadcast to you. No exception."

He kissed her for a long time. When he pulled back, his eyes glistened. "I love you, Ana. Stay safe."

She grabbed him for a tight hug. "I love you, too, Sawyer. You're the one who needs to stay safe. When do you leave?"

"Soon."

She sighed as tears streamed down her face. "Please come back to me."

"I will. I promise. This is such a routine mission, I'll be bored and calling you all the time wanting to talk and you'll be saying, 'Sawyer. I have to practice,' and I'll say, 'Great. I'll listen," and I will."

With a final kiss that tasted salty from their tears, they separated. Sawyer followed her on his bike into San Diego before peeling off for Coronado. That made her cry harder.

As soon as she returned, Randall upped her practice time, explaining she'd lost an entire week. He was still furious about having to reschedule her San Diego tour, but he'd been able to move a few things and get her dates rescheduled for late October.

She didn't hear from Sawyer for almost a week, the seven longest days of her life. When he finally called, he was in Africa, but that's all he told her. He mostly wanted to talk about her and her upcoming concertos.

A few times, while she practiced, he put his phone on speaker to let his team listen. Loud applause and whistles accompanied the end of each piece, which made her smile.

For the next four weeks, she traveled for her sched-uled appearances. She left the U.S. to play in France, and was shocked to meet Sawyer's parents, who'd come from Belgium to hear her. His folks had been wonderful. They'd seemed genuinely happy about the marriage, unlike her own family.

Her father continued his support, but he had warned her that her Grandmother Zeller was not happy

Her mother, with encouragement from Ana's

Grandmother Zeller, had contacted a lawyer. First about an annulment. When Ana told the lawyer to get lost, their second action was to get a postnuptial agreement. Ana decided to ignore them. Sawyer was untouchable in Africa. When he returned, she'd make a point of tearing up all the paperwork in front of both women.

Her chats with Sawyer, when he wasn't listening to her playing, were intimate. Sometimes, he would tell her what he wanted to do to her when he got back. His voice and his dirty talk made her horny. Who'd have thought it? Ana Cristiano loved sex and could have orgasms, but only with Sawyer. There wasn't another man anywhere who could make her wet and achy with just his words.

It was early October when she finally had a break. Instead of going to her parents' home in Chicago, she took a room in Seattle overlooking the ocean. She'd always loved water. Now, the sound of the ocean waves made her feel closer to Sawyer.

Plus, Geoffrey had recently bought a house there. He had an excellent grand piano she could use to practice during her tour break, another activity that made her feel closer to Sawyer.

She flipped on the television to surf for a movie. The television was set to a news channel. She joined in the middle of an ongoing story about Africa. As she half-way listened, the report talked about the crash of a military Black Hawk helicopter delivering a team of Navy SEALs on a mission.

Ana's head snapped toward the television. Her heart leapt into her throat. Sawyer!

"Unfortunately, there were no survivors, other than

the co-pilot. Names are being withheld until notif-ication of the next-of-kin."

Ana's breathing became a hard pant. Her heart raced. Her arms grew numb. A heart attack. At only thirty, she was having a heart attack. She didn't care. Without Sawyer, life wasn't worth living. She toppled off the couch onto the floor.

ANA BECAME AWARE OF RHYMICAL BEEPING AND whispered voices. Someone pried open her eye and flashed a bright light. She didn't like heaven, or was this hell?

"Stop it," she said. "That hurts."

"And there she is," an unfamiliar voice said.

Ana opened her eyes to slits. The man leaning over her was a stranger.

"Ana, are you okay?"

She rolled her head toward the voice. Geoffrey was sitting beside her bed.

"Where am I? What am I doing here?"

"You're at Seattle General Emergency Department," the stranger said.

"Who are you?"

The man smiled. "Dr. Latture. You fainted."

"No, I never faint."

"Well then, today's my lucky day. I get to treat your first one."

Geoffrey stepped up to the side of her bed. "You scared the crap out of me."

"What are you doing here?"

"I flew to Seattle to talk to you. Dad is retiring at

the end of the year, and I wanted you to hear that from me."

"Fine, whatever. What are you doing here?" She gestured around the room.

"I was outside your door at the inn and I heard something thump on the floor. When you didn't answer, I got security to unlock your door. I found you on the floor and called an ambulance."

"What's wrong with me?" But even as the words left her mouth, she remembered Sawyer. Dead. Oh my God. She began to cry.

"You're fine," Dr. Latture said and glanced toward Geoffrey. "Is this man your husband?"

"No!" they both replied simultaneously.

"I'm a friend," Geoffrey said. "Do you need me to step out of the room?"

"Please. I'd like to speak with Ms. Cristiano privately."

When they were alone, the doctor said, "Have you had these fainting spells before?"

"No, never." She struggled upright. "I'm fine. Geoffrey overreacted." She paused and asked, "Am I pregnant? I know pregnant women faint."

Dr. Latture shook his head. "No, you're not. Did you think you were?"

She shrugged and tears began to run down her cheeks. "I'd hoped. You checked that?"

Of course, she'd hoped she was pregnant. At least she would have had a piece of the man she'd fallen so in love with. Now, she'd have only her memories, and she didn't have enough of those.

The doctor nodded. "When you were admitted, and the test was negative. I'm sorry."

"Can I leave?"

"I'd like you to stay overnight, just observation."

She tossed back the sheet. "No. I need to go. Can you call Geoffrey back into the room?"

Geoffrey walked back in as she was struggling to stand. "Ana. Get back in bed."

"I need my phone. I need to call Sawyer."

"Okay, but get back in bed."

"No. I'm going back to the hotel. Can you stay with me?"

"I'd rather she stays here overnight," Dr. Latture said. "But as long as someone is with her, I'll discharge her."

"I'll stay," Geoffrey said.

The doctor left the room, and Ana sat back on the bed.

"My phone, Geoffrey."

"I don't have it, Ana." He held out his. "You can use mine."

She snatched it from his hands and dialed Sawyer's phone. It rang until his voice mail picked up. "Sawyer. Call me. I need to hear from you."

Geoffrey took his phone. "What is going on, Ana?"

"You heard about the helicopter crash in Africa?"

"Sure, it's all over the news. It was shot down, not just crashed. The Pentagon is threatening all kinds of retaliation. Why?"

"Sawyer's in Africa."

"So? It was a helicopter of Navy SEALs."

"Sawyer's a SEAL."

Geoffrey's eyes opened wide. "Oh. I didn't know. I knew he was military, but that's all Dad said. I'm sorry. You think he was on that copter?"

"Yes. I haven't heard from him in a couple of days,

but that's not unexpected. It happens. But now? I can't reach him."

Another man entered the room. "I got us lattes, is that okay?"

Ana frowned and looked at Geoffrey. "Who is this?"

"Oh, sorry. This is Linden, my, um friend."

Linden handed a coffee to Geoffrey, and said, "It's time, Geoff. I refuse to keep our relationship hidden as though it was something to be ashamed of. I'm not ashamed of you. I hope you feel the same." He turned toward Ana, and said, "I'm his boyfriend."

Ana grinned for the first time. "I'm so happy to meet you, Linden."

Geoffrey's face was bright red. "I…didn't… um…Dad…"

Ana held up her hand. "You can tell Randall whatever you want to, Geoffrey. I'm just glad you found someone you care for. That's all I could want for you."

His face relaxed. "Thank you." He looked at Linden. "We're taking her back to our house for tonight."

"Cool," Linden said. "Happy to have her."

"You don't have to do that," Ana protested. "I'll be fine. I'm sure Sawyer will call me tonight."

"We'll get your phone and take it with us."

Sawyer didn't call that night, nor any night for the next two weeks. No one from the military contacted her, but then maybe they didn't know about the marriage and had contacted his parents instead.

But wouldn't they have contacted her?

She tried to call him every night. There was never an answer other than his voice message asking her to leave a message.

Relenting, she called his parents numerous times, and never got an answer from them either.

In desperation, she called Patty, praying her husband could find out something. But she hit a dead-end there as well. Neither had heard a word.

She'd watched their wedding video so many times, she knew every word, every scene. She spent hours looking at their pictures. She'd been so shocked when she'd seen him standing there with short hair, a clean face, and in an immaculate dress blue uniform. He'd told her later that Paul had brought it with him.

She'd thought Sawyer sexy before, but clean-shaven Sawyer almost made her drop her roses…six for each day they'd been together. She'd thought him handsome, but that word didn't begin to describe him. He'd been handsome, and gorgeous, and sexy, and the most beautiful vision her eyes had ever beheld. She'd almost run across the living room to get to him.

And those nights together? He'd ruined her for any other man. She'd never want another.

She was happy for Geoffrey and Linden. Linden was perfect for him, and was obviously in love with Geoffrey. She hoped they found their happily ever after like she had, even if her ever after was gone.

After two weeks, she knew beyond a doubt; Sawyer had died in that crash. She'd never see him again. She'd never kiss his beautiful lips; never run her tongue down his abdomen and listen to his hiss.

She was broken. Her life would never be the same after Sawyer Beckett.

THE RESCHEDULED DATES FOR SAN DIEGO CAME. SHE wanted to cancel, but she couldn't do that to her audience again. She had inconvenienced the musicians in the orchestra previously, and she refused to do it a second time. She had no choice but to go on tonight.

She sent two tickets to Patty. She came and brought her sister. Ana tried to be a gracious host, but seeing Patty brought back all her wedding memories. Patty had hugged her, told her to break a leg, but not literally, she'd added with a laugh, and the ladies had gone to find their seats.

She was avoiding her mother. While her mother hadn't been gleeful that Sawyer was dead, she hadn't been all that remorseful for her attitude and actions toward him. Someday in the future, Ana might speak with her mother again, but not anytime soon.

Ana did talk with her father, who provided the right words of comfort and support she needed. He understood why she couldn't come home. He loved Ana's mother, but that didn't stop his being extremely irritated with her.

A knock on her door pulled her away from her musings. "Yes?"

"Five minutes, Ms. Cristiano."

"Thank you." Ana flexed her fingers and got ready to perform what she suspected would be the hardest concerto of her life.

She stood, took a deep breath, and walked to the wings to wait for her cue to enter. The conductor looked over his musicians and nodded. Then he looked at Ana. She walked out to the grand piano sitting front and center on the stage. The orchestra sat behind her, filling the large stage. As was her habit, she sat her phone on the piano, dialed Sawyer's phone, and let it ring. When his voice mail answered, she sat the phone on a small table beside her piano, and nodded to the conductor. Even if he would never hear her play again, she played for him, and only him.

The orchestra began. She placed her hands on the piano keys and played, pouring all her sadness and emotions into the keys. She pounded the keys with a virtuosity that poured from her soul. Her music had never sounded like this before. She rocked on her seat, closed her eyes, and let her fingers take over her body.

At the end of Beethoven's Piano Sonata Number Nine in B Major, the first piece of the evening, the audience applauded loudly, which wasn't typical of her usual audience. She usually got a polite clapping as they waited for the next piece to begin. She played through the next six pieces, each one more remarkable than the previous one.

Her heart was on fire, crying out for the man she'd lost. Her soul wept all over her keyboard. Her audience had no idea they were watching her dissolve into nothing but black musical notes.

She'd been dreading the seventh piece of the evening. Rachmaninoff's Concerto Number Three, her solo piece and her and Sawyer's song, the one she'd played for him on the night they'd married. She'd wanted to ask for it to be removed, but in the end, she couldn't bring herself to ask. She had to learn to go on.

Her fingers rested on the keys waiting for the conductor to signal for her to begin. When he did, she forgot the world around her and played. She didn't watch her hands as she played. Tonight's music came from her soul, not her fingers.

She was ten minutes into the concerto when she glanced into the wings. Her fingers stopped. Her eyes opened wide. Her heart jumped into her throat as tears poured down her face. Was Sawyer really there or was this a hallucination? Was she losing her mind?

She stood but found she couldn't move.

A murmur rippled through the audience. She heard them, but she couldn't process what she was seeing or hearing.

"Sawyer?" she said quietly. "Sawyer?" she repeated louder.

Her hallucination took a step forward and blew her a kiss.

"Sawyer!" she cried and ran toward the stage's wing where he stood.

He jogged out and met her halfway. Picking her up in his arms, he kissed her.

"I thought you were dead," she said with a voice choked with tears.

"We went on total blackout after the raid that killed Zulu team. I am so sorry. There was no way to reach you and tell you. No one could call home. I am so sorry." Tears rolled down his face. "I love you so much. I never wanted to cause you any pain. I am so sorry. Forgive me."

"There's nothing to forgive. You promised to come back to me, and you have. I love you so much."

Noise from the audience drew her attention. She turned and smiled. "Ladies and gentlemen. Let me introduce you to my husband, Petty Officer First Class, Sawyer Beckett. I'm afraid he surprised me this evening. I wasn't expecting him…" She wiped her tears. "As you can see. Help me welcome him home."

The applause from the audience was loud and raucous, definitely not what she was used to.

Sawyer waved, and then kissed her. "Finish. We can talk later."

She smiled and nodded.

He walked into the wings and turned to watch her as she retook her place at the piano. The conductor looked at her with a raised eyebrow.

"Let's continue," she said, and began her solo again, except this time, she played for an audience of only one.

No matter how many people she played for the rest of her life, the only audience who mattered stood in the wings, his legs spread wide in his stance, and his arms crossed over his chest.

Her audience of one would always be enough to carry her for the rest of her life.

EPILOGUE

A Note from Sawyer Beckett
    One Year Later

Hi! This is Sawyer Beckett. Thank you for reading my story about how I met my wife and tricked her into marrying me. I know I'm a lucky man. Not only did I marry the most incredible woman, damned if she doesn't love me, too. Never thought it was possible to be this happy.

I'd never understood how my mother was content to follow my father from base to base, state to state, country to country, and be happy. Now, I get it. I thought she didn't have roots, so I didn't have roots, but the roots were always there right in front of me. Dad was "the roots" of our family. Home was where Dad was. I get that now. My home is wherever my beloved wife is.

When the Zulu team was shot down, the entire African military component went on total communications blackout. We were there, and are still there, to support and train. It was unusual for the U.S. military to be part of active fighting. But it does happen and it happened that day. The SEALs lost an excellent unit of men, all fine and upstanding SEALs. I had served with Zulu and knew the unit. It was a tragic loss to the military professionally, and to me personally.

When we were sent back to the U.S., I tried unsuccessfully to call Ana. I should have called Paul to reach out to her, but it didn't occur to me. I'm not used to having someone waiting at home for my safe return.

Ana's mother was a pain in my ass for a while. The day Irene and her mother showed up at our house with the postnuptial paperwork, Ana laughed her ass off, and tore the pages into confetti. I would've signed the damn thing because I'm never letting Ana go, so it didn't matter to me one way or the other.

I will confess to being a tad shocked to discover Ana had so much money she needed a prenup. Of course, the over-the-top wedding and honeymoon suite should have tipped me off, but I was so in love with her that I didn't look too close at the trappings. Plus, she kept swearing hotel management had comped a lot of the expenses. To this day, I don't know if that's true or not, and I don't care.

But we did give in to her mother on one item.

On the Friday before Thanksgiving, we replayed our wedding video for a group of her friends and social connections, followed by the most ridiculous reception you can imagine. Live music. Open bar. Flowing champagne. Lobster. Prime rib. A wedding cake that made me laugh.

The cake was white and elegant on one side with roses and a swag, like how I suspect Irene saw her daughter.

However, when the cake was turned, each layer had

been decorated with a Navy motif. The bottom layer was in Navy colors. The Navy SEAL emblem decorated the top layer. On the middle layer, the baker had drawn a frog holding a trident.

We cut the cake with my sword, which Ana had loved. Of course, she ran around with it all night trying to "knight" our guests. No heads were lost in her endeavors, however.

Before you ask, yes, I did retire from the Navy. Not because Ana has an obscene amount of money and we didn't need my salary. Again, I didn't care then and I don't care now. No, I retired to travel with her as she continues to tour and make records.

Randall did retire at the end of the year as Geoffrey had told Ana. We talked about it and decided to let Geoffrey take over where his dad left off. Geoffrey knows all the ins and outs of the business, even if I'm sure he's still a little jealous of Ana's talent.

Geoffrey and Linden are getting married in the spring. As Ana had suspected, Geoffrey was being pushed by his father to marry her. Randall had been sure Geoffrey's sexual orientation would hamper his career as Ana's manager. Ana and Sawyer both agreed that was ridiculous, and it turned out they were right. Nobody cared about Geoffrey's love life; they only cared about scheduling Ana to play for them…at some nonsensical low payment. Yeah, that never worked. If anything, Geoffrey was tougher to deal with than his father, and Ana's popularity only increased with each rise in her asking price.

She still plays concertos, but she's hooked up with some country musicians for some experimental songs. So far, she's loving the experience in Nashville and the reception from the public to the new music has been positive. She's the only one who's surprised by that. I'm not. I know my wife can do anything she wants to. And she knows I'm here for life. I'll support her in any endeavor.

If the day comes that she wants to quit, I'll support her in that.

If the day comes she wants a baby, I'll support her in that also.

Until then, we'll continue to practice…both the piano and the baby-making.

Sawyer

FROM THE AUTHOR

Thanks for reading Hot SEAL, Labor Day. I love my readers. Without you, I wouldn't be here.

Readers are always asking: What can I do to help you?

My answer is always the same: PLEASE give me an honest review. Every review helps.

Also, I have a reader group (D'Alba D'Arlings) where I get readers for Advanced Reader Copies. If you are interested in joining us, shoot me an email at cynthia@cynthiadalba.com The group is Facebook based for reader convenience.

Thank you again for buying my book. On to the next adventure!

Cynthia

Acknowledgments

First, a big THANK YOU and hug to Delilah Devlin for working overtime on edits for this book. Love you.

Second. I couldn't have done this without my beta readers who stopped what they were doing to read and give me comments and edits. Whew, ladies. I know I put a lot pressure on you so THANK YOU very much! Here are their names: Debbie Watson, Pamela Reveal, Teresa Fordice, Brenda Rumsey, Jill Duffy Purinton, Missi Adams Metz, and Jennie Grunden Fortna. Any errors found are solely my fault.

To Mandy Harbin - Thanks for letting me use your name as owner of the cabins.

To Parker Kincade - I hope you enjoyed your "personal" lake!

ABOUT THE AUTHOR

 New York Times and USA Today Bestselling author Cynthia D'Alba started writing on a challenge from her husband in 2006 and discovered having imaginary sex with lots of hunky men was fun. She was born and raised in a small Arkansas town. After being gone for a number of years, she's thrilled to be making her home back in Arkansas living in a vine-covered cottage on the banks of an eight-thousand acre lake. When she's not reading or writing or plotting, she's doorman for her border collie, cook, housekeeper and chief bottle washer for her husband and slave to a noisy, messy parrot. She loves to chat online with friends and fans.

You can find her most days at one of the following online homes:

Website: cynthiadalba.com
Facebook:Facebook/cynthiadalba
Twitter:@cynthiadalba
Pinterest: Pinterest/CynthiaDAlba
Newsletter:NewsletterSign-Up
Reader Group: D'Alba D'Arlings
Or drop her a line at cynthia@cynthiadalba.com

Or send snail mail to: Cynthia D'Alba PO Box 2116
Hot Springs, AR 71914

ALSO BY CYNTHIA D'ALBA

Hot SEAL, Confirmed Bachelor

Hot SEAL, Secret Service (novella)

Hot SEAL, Sweet & Spicy

Hot SEAL, Labor Day

Brotherhood Protectors

(Part of Elle James Brotherhood Series)

Texas Ranger Rescue

Texas Marine Mayhem

Read on for excerpts from
other Hot SEAL books
by
Cynthia D'Alba

Hot SEAL, Black Coffee
A Dallas Debutante/SEALs in Paradise/McCool
Trilogy (Book 1)

Dealing with a sexy ex-girlfriend, a jewel heist, and a murder-for-hire can make an ex-SEAL bodyguard a tad cranky.

Trevor Mason accepts what should be a simple job…protect the jewels his ex-girlfriend will wear to a breast cancer fundraiser. As founder and owner of Eye Spy International, he should send one of his guys, but he needs to get his ex out of his system and this is the perfect opportunity to remind himself that she is a spoiled, rich debutante who dumped him with a Dear John letter during his SEAL training.

Respected breast cancer doctor Dr. Risa McCool hates being in the limelight for her personal life. Her life's work is breast cancer treatment and research, which she'd rather be known for than for her carefree, partying debutante years. She agrees to be the chairperson for the annual breast cancer fundraiser even though it means doing publicity appearances and interviews, all while wearing the famous pink Breast

Cancer Diamond for each public event. The multi-million dollar value of the pink stone requires an armed bodyguard at all times.

Past attractions flame, proving to be a distraction to the serious reality of the situation. When Risa and the millions in diamonds go missing, nothing will stop Trevor from bringing her home, with or without the jewels.

At two-thirty Monday afternoon, Dr. Risa McCool's world shifted on its axis. He was back. She wasn't ready. But then, would she ever be ready?

Four hours passed before she was able to disengage from work and go home. As she pulled under the portico of her high-rise building and the condo valet hurried out to park her eight-year-old sedan, her stomach roiled at the realization that Trevor Mason—high school and college boyfriend and almost fiancé—would be waiting for her in her condo, or at least should be. She pressed a shaking hand to her abdomen and inhaled a deep, calming breath. It didn't work. There was still a slight quiver to her hands as she grabbed her purse and briefcase from the passenger seat.

She paused to look in the mirror. A tired brunette looked back at her. Dark circles under her eyes. Limp hair pulled into a ponytail at the back of her head. Pale lips. Paler cheeks. Not one of her better looks.

Would he be the same? Tall with sun-kissed hair and mesmerizing azure-blue eyes?

Tall, sure. That was a given.

Eye color would have to be the same, but his sun-bleached hair? His muscular physique? In high school and college, he'd played on the offense for their high school and college football teams, but she had never really understood what he did. Sometimes he ran and sometimes he hit other guys. What she remembered were strong arms and a wide chest. Would those be the same?

Almost fifteen years had passed since she'd last seen him. He hadn't come back for their tenth nor their fifteenth high school reunions. The explanation for his absences involved SEAL missions to who knew where. Risa had wondered if she'd ever see him again, whether he'd make it through all his deployments and secret ops.

Well, he had and now she had to work with him.

She took a deep breath and slid from the car.

"Good Evening, Dr. McCool," the valet said.

"Evening, John. Do you know if my guest arrived?"

"Yes, ma'am. About four hours ago."

"Do you know if the groceries were delivered?"

"Yes, ma'am. Cleaning service has also been in."

"Thank you. Have a nice evening."

"You, too."

She acknowledged the guard on duty at the desk with a nod and continued to the private residents-only elevator that opened to a back-door entrance to her condo. After putting her key in the slot, she pressed the button for the forty-first floor and then leaned against the wall for the ride.

Her anxiety at seeing Trevor climbed as the elevator dinged past each floor. It was possible, even probable, that she had made a mistake following her mother's advice to employ his company. She was required to have a bodyguard for every public event since the announcement of the pink Breast Cancer Diamond. Her insurance company insisted on it. The jewelry designer demanded it. And worse, her mother was adamant on a guard. How did one say no to her mother?

Plus, as head of the Dallas Area Breast Cancer Research Center, she'd been tasked with wearing that gaudy necklace with a pink diamond big enough to choke a horse for the annual fundraising gala. The damn thing was worth close to fifteen or twenty million and was heavy as hell. Who'd want it?

The elevator dinged one last time and the doors slid open. She stepped into a small vestibule and let herself into her place expecting to see Trevor.

Only, she didn't.

Instead there was music—jazz to be specific. She followed the sounds of Stan Getz to her balcony, her heart in her throat.

A man sat in a recliner facing the night lights of Dallas, a highball in one hand, a cigar in the other.

"I'm glad to see you stock the good bourbon," he said, lifting the glass, but not turning to face her. "And my brand, too. Should I be impressed?"

Her jaw clenched. Their fights had always been about money—what she had and what he didn't.

"I don't know," she said. "Are you impressed?"

He took a drag off the cigar and chased the smoke down his throat with a gulp of hundred-dollar bourbon. "Naw. You can afford it."

"Are you going to look at me or will my first

conversation with you in fifteen years be with the back of your head?"

After stabbing out the cigar, he finished his drink, sat it on the tile floor, and rose. Lord, he was still as towering and overwhelming as she remembered him. At five-feet-ten-inches, Risa was tall, but Trevor's height made her feel positively petite. As he turned, every muscle in her body tensed as she stood unsure whether she was preparing to fight him, flee from him or fuck him.

"Hello, Risa."

HOT SEAL, COLD BEER
DIAMOND LAKES, TEXAS BOOK 2

An ex-Navy SEAL agrees to play fake lover for the Maid of Honor at a destination wedding only to discover that what happens on a Caribbean Island can sometimes follow you home.

Nicholas Falcone, aka Nikko, aka Falcon, is five months out from active SEAL duty, putting his pre-service accounting degree to use while going to law school at night. He'd love to take a vacation between semesters, but every buck is earmarked for his education. When a fellow accountant approaches him about his sister needing an escort for a destination wedding, Nikko jumps at the idea. With the wedding families footing the bill, what does he have to lose?

Surgeon Dr. Jennifer Pierce is still stinging from a broken engagement. Going to a destination wedding at the Sand Castle Resort in the Caribbean would be great if only her ex-fiancé and his new wife weren't also attending. Her options are to find a date or not go, but not going isn't really an option. That means letting her brother set her up with a guy from his accounting office…Heaven forbid. When did accountants start looking like this?

** Cold Beer ** is part of the Diamond Lakes, Texas Series and Sand Castle Resort series. Each book can be read as a stand-alone. They do not have cliffhanger endings.

Hot SEAL, Cold Beer is also in the "SEALs in Paradise" connected series. Each book in the multi-author branded SEALs in Paradise series can be read stand-alone, and individual books do not have to be read in any particular order.

Read on for an excerpt:

If there was one thing Dr. Jennifer Pierce hated, it was not being in control. She'd rather tell people what to do than be told. She despised surprises and was much more comfortable in situations where she had all the information. And, most importantly, she maintained a firm discipline over all emotions, especially her own.

However, right now, she was as nervous as a first-year med student holding a scalpel in surgery, and that irritated her, which only amped up her anxiety.

She agitated the martini shaker violently, the ice clanging against the stainless-steel container like a hail storm. After pouring the dry martini into a glass, she took a long, steadying sip.

Yeah, that didn't help her nerves.

On the other hand, the stiff drink didn't hurt, either.

With a resigned sigh, she walked to the living room and sat to await Nicholas Falcone. Her brother, Robert, had suggested Falcone as her potential date for a fast-approaching destination wedding. She loved her twin brother and trusted him...mostly. Because historically, the men he believed perfect for her had been so far off the mark as to be not even in the same book, much less on the same page. But she was between a rock and a slab of granite.

All she knew about this Falcone guy was he worked at McKenzie, Gladwell and Associates with her brother and had been a Navy SEAL. Weren't they called jarheads? Hell, she didn't know. She took another gulp of the cold vodka. What she knew about the military wouldn't fill a shot glass.

She'd give her brother credit for one thing. If Falcone's online photo was anywhere accurate, Nicholas Falcone looked the part she needed him to play. When Robert had called her to tell her about his solution to her dateless dilemma, she'd pulled up her brother's accounting firm on the internet to look at the staff photos and had been pleasantly surprised. The picture had been of a gorgeous guy with a neatly trimmed beard, a sexy smile, and mischievous eyes. Man, she hoped he could carry on a decent conversation and not grunt answers to everything.

Her doorbell pealed, and her heart jumped in response. Pressing her hand over her quaking stomach, she drew in a calming breath, not that a calming breath had ever helped. So she took the next best option to deep breathing and finished off her martini.

Carrying her empty glass with her, she opened the

door and looked at her potential blind date. Her brain hiccuped or maybe quit functioning altogether. He didn't look at all like she'd expected and prepared for. In person, he was…more. A whole lot more. With his chiseled cheeks and sharp chin, he was a million times more attractive in real life. His green eyes—a billion times more beautiful than that black-and-white photo showed—held an amused twinkle that coordinated handsomely with his amused smile. And his body? Dear lord. Broad shoulders pulled a white, oxford shirt tightly across them. Long sleeves rolled to mid-forearm exposed thick, ropey muscles that bunched and flexed when he extended his hand.

"Dr. Pierce. I'm Nikko Falcone."

She stepped back, embarrassed that she'd been staring at him. "Of course. I'm sorry. I was…never mind. Not important. Come in."

He lowered his hand and stepped into her foyer. The roomy area shrank. She'd expected tall and well-built, but the degree of just how brawny he was registered with a clunk upside her head.

Taking a step back, she gestured with her martini glass. "I'm having a drink. Can I fix you something?"

"A cold beer, if you have one."

"Sure. Have a seat." She flipped her hand toward the living room.

Beer in her refrigerator wasn't the norm. She wasn't much of a beer drinker, but since she hadn't known much about Nicholas Falcone's drink preferences—or anything at all about him really—she'd stocked a six-pack of beer as well as red wine, white wine, and the makings for any mixed drink imaginable. Always prepared, was her motto.

She would have made a hell of a boy scout.

She pulled out a cold bottle, cracked off the top, and got a chilled beer stein from her freezer. While she was there, she also poured herself a fresh vodka martini. Realizing she had too many items and not enough hands, she loaded everything on a tray and went back to the living room.

"I brought you a glass," she said, setting the tray on the glass coffee table in front of him. She lifted her martini and took the chair across from him.

"Bottle's fine," he said and took a long draw off the bottle.

She hid her discomfort with his drinking beer straight from the bottle. The people at the destination wedding they would be attending ran in high-society circles. Beer from bottles had been fine back in college, but now that they were all in their thirties, she was sure her friends, like her, had progressed to more sophisticated drinks and glasses.

Mentally, she made a note to talk with him about appearances.

He leaned back on her white sofa, stretched his arm across the back, and crossed an ankle over his knee. That's when she saw a tattoo peeking out from where the sleeve of his white oxford had been rolled up. From this distance, she could make out tines. A trident? As a doctor, she knew all about the infections that went with tattoos, and she wanted to disapprove. Instead, she got a little turned on. She didn't like that, or she shouldn't like that.

Damn. He had her all confused.

"So," she said, trying to gather her wits and the reins to the conversation. "What did Robert tell you?"

"In a nutshell, you had a fiancé. A big-time corporate lawyer. Said legal-eagle dirtbag got his secretary pregnant. Married her. Dumped you when he got back from his honeymoon. That about right?"

She winced. "In a nutshell."

He lifted the bottle to his lips—which she couldn't help notice were full and soft. Of course she noticed. She was a doctor. She always observed the human body...especially one like this.

He swallowed. His Adam's apple rose and fell with the action.

She had to get her air conditioning fixed. This room was too warm.

Hot SEAL, Alaskan Nights
A SEALs in Paradise Novel

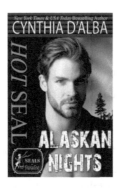

From NYT and USA Today Best Selling Author comes a beach read that isn't the typical sun-drenched location. Homer, Alaska. A Navy SEAL on leave. A nurse practitioner in seclusion. A jealous ex-lover looking for redemption...or is it revenge?

Navy SEAL Levi Van der Hayden, aka Dutch, returns to his family home in Homer, AK for the three Rs...rest, relaxation and recovery. As the only SEAL injured during his team's last mission, the last thing he wants to do is show his bullet wound to friends...it's in his left gluteus maximus and he's tired of being the butt of all the jokes (his own included.)

After a violent confrontation with a controlling, narcissistic ex-lover, nurse practitioner Bailey Brown flees Texas for Alaska. A maternal grandmother still in residence provides her with the ideal sanctuary...still in the U.S. but far enough away to escape her ex's reach.

Attracted to the cute nurse from his welcome home beach party, Levi insists on showing her the real

Alaska experience. When her safety is threatened, he must use all his SEAL skills to protect her and eliminate the risk, even if it means putting his own life on the line.

Levi Van der Hayden's left butt cheek was on fire. He shifted uncomfortably in the back seat of the subcompact car masquerading as their Uber ride. As soon as he moved, the stitches in his left thigh reminded him that pushing off with that leg was also mistake.

"We should try to get upgraded when we get to the airport," Compass said.

Compass, also known as Levi's best friend Rio North, was going way out of his way to help Levi get home leave, but at this moment, Levi gritted his teeth at the ridiculous suggestion.

"I don't have the money for that and you know it." Levi, aka Dutch to his SEAL team buds, knew he shouldn't be so grumpy what with all Compass was doing for him but damn it! Why did he have to be shot in the ass? The guys would never let him live it down.

He repositioned his hips so most of the weight was on his uninjured right butt cheek.

"You bring anything for the pain, Dutch?"

"Took something about an hour ago, which right now seems like last week."

The car stopped at the Departure gates of San Diego International Airport. Dutch climbed from the back seat of the way-too-tiny car with a few choice cuss words and stood on the sidewalk. Compass paid the driver and then hefted out two duffle bags. After slinging both onto his shoulders, he gestured toward the airport with his chin.

Once inside, Compass said, "Seriously Dutch, you need to upgrade. There is no way you are going to be able to stretch out and you know what the doctor said about pulling those stitches."

Levi glared at his friend and answered him with a one-finger response.

Compass grinned back him. "All joking aside, I'll pay for your upgrade. Your ass literally *needs* to be in first class." The asshole then leaned back and glanced down at Levi's ass...well actually the cheek where he'd been shot coming back from their last fucking mission.

"No, damn it, Compass, I already told you I can't afford it and I'm not accepting charity." Levi knew his friend could afford to upgrade Levi to a big, roomy, first-class seat, but he was already taking Compass way out of his way with this trip. When his friend opened his mouth to speak, Levi held up a hand to stop him. "Not even from you. I appreciate it, man, I really do, but no." Levi shook his head emphatically. "I fucking hate being such a pain in your ass, har har har."

To say Levi had been the target of his SEAL team buddies' relentless butt jokes would be an understatement. They'd been brutal in the way only people who love you can. Levi knew that. Understood that. And would have been there throwing out the butt and ass jokes if it'd been anyone else who'd gotten shot in the ass, but it wasn't. It was him and he was tired of it. He lowered himself carefully onto a bench.

Compass looked around and then back to Levi. "Okay, look, I'm going to go talk to the agent over there. I'm not spending a dime, but sometimes they let active duty get upgrades. Let me see what I can do. Okay?"

Levi followed Compass's gaze to an attractive brunette behind the Delta service counter. He chuckled. "Damn man, you could pick up a woman anywhere, couldn't you?"

Compass shrugged, but his grin said he knew exactly what Levi was talking about. "It's a God-given talent. But that's not what this is about. Give me your military ID."

Levi pulled out his card, but hesitated. Compass had more money than God, Dropping an thousand or so dollars to change a plane ticket was probably pocket change to him, but not to Levi.

Compass jerked Levi's military card out his hand with a snort. "Shit that damaged ass muscle has fucked up your reflexes."

"Fuck you, man. It's the pain meds." Levi narrowed his eyes at his best friend. "Not a penny, Compass, not a fucking penny. Got it?"

"Loud and clear." Compass pointed to him. "Stay here and look pathetic."

Compass had only taken a few steps before Levi heard him laugh. God damn asshole.

Jesus, he hated this. Not only was he in pain, but the damn doctors had restricted him from lifting anything over twenty pounds. Twenty pounds! Like he was some fucking girl or something. He was a Navy SEAL. He could lift twenty pounds with his toes…or could before just moving his toes made the exit wound on his thigh ache.

Now that their last mission was behind them—he groaned at his own bad joke—the team had a little time off, which meant he could finally go home for a few days. However, the restrictions from the doctors meant someone had to help him with his duffle bag since it definitely weighed more than twenty pounds. He was pissed off and embarrassed by that limit to his activities. Hell, even jogging was off his activities list until the stitches healed a little more.

He'd been ordered to do medical follow-up at the Alaskan VA Health Clinic. Knowing his commander, Skipper would follow up on that, and if Levi didn't follow orders, his ass would be grass. He groan again and ordered himself to stop with the ass jokes.

Turning his attention back to the action across the lobby Levi watched Compass operate. He was too far away to hear the conversation, but he knew his friend's M.O. well. He'd smile. He'd compliment the woman. Then he'd toss in his best friend's war wound for sympathy. Levi snorted to himself. He'd seen Compass in action too many times to count.

Compass leaned toward the Delta agent and Levi was sure the poor woman had been sucked into Compass's charismatic gravitational pull. She didn't stand a chance against a pro like Compass.

When Compass set both of their duffle bags on the scale and the airline agent tagged them, Levi was at least sure he was going home. What he didn't know was if it would be in the front of the plane or the back of the plane. If it weren't for his ass and leg, he wouldn't care where he sat, but he knew that wasn't true for his friend, who always went first-class when he could.

Compass turned from the check-in desk and

started toward Levi with a broad smile he'd seen before when Compass got what he wanted.

Levi eyed him. "Why do you have a shit-eating grin on your face? What did you do?"

"I'm smiling because I'm a fucking magic man." He handed Levi a boarding pass.

Levi studied the boarding pass with first class all in capital letters. "Did you buy this?" His lips tightened into a straight line.

Compass help up his hands. "Nope. Not a penny spent. I swear on my mother's grave."

"Your mother is alive, asshole."

"Yeah, but we have a family plot and we all have real estate allotted. I swear *I* didn't spend a single dime on that ticket man. That pretty little thing over there hooked you up." He motioned over to Brittany who was busy with another customer.

"Sir, are you ready?"

Levi's gaze fell on an attendant pushing a wheelchair. "What the fuck?"

Hot SEAL, Confirmed Bachelor
A SEALs in Paradise Novel

When a Navy SEAL runs into an obstacle, he climbs over it, under it, around it, or destroys it. So what if it's a woman?

Master Chief Benjamin Blackwell has it all. Adventure, good looks, skills, and women. His life is perfect and he has no intention of changing a thing. Until *her*.

Holly Maxwell is a sexy woman unlike anyone he's met before. A widow for ten years, she's happy with her life even with the trials of raising a pre-teen daughter, and being the only girl in a nosy, boisterous family of Coronado cops.

But what makes her so inexplicable to this Navy SEAL is her total lack of interest in *him*.

"What can I get you ladies?" the server asked as she set cardboard coasters on the table.

"I've got this," Bethany said. "Bring us one, no wait, two pitchers of margaritas-on -the-rocks, and two tequila shots each."

"Are you kidding me?" Holly asked. "Shots?"

Bethany waved her off. "Make that Herradura Silver for those shots."

"You got it," the woman said. "My name's Liz. Be back."

The woman walked toward the bar to place the order.

"First, shots?" Holly asked. "And second, dropping tequila names?"

Bethany laughed. "Trust me. This is sipping tequila. You'll love it. Besides, it's our first night out as family sisters. We are cel-e-brat-ting."

"Remember, I'm driving," Holly said.

"No problem. We'll get you home if you can't drive."

Liz returned. "Okay, ladies. Here we go. Two pitchers of margaritas-on-the-rocks and six shots of Herradura Silver." She set empty margarita glasses on the table. "What else can I get for you?"

"I think we're good," Bethany said. She picked up the pitcher and filled each glass. Then she lifted hers in a toast. "To having the sisters I've always wanted in my life."

"Awww," Holly said and fake sniffed. She clinked her glass to Bethany's.

"You say that now," Diana joked. "Just wait until we

drop the boys at your house for the weekend. Then, let's hear what you have to say about family."

The three women toasted with laughter and drank.

That was only the first toast. For the next hour, every freshly poured drink started a new round of toasts. As Bethany had warned, Holly found that the tequila shots slid down her throat like melted butter. Smooth and tasty.

The first round of pitchers and shots lasted almost an hour. Diana offered to buy the next round. After a serious discussion, the ladies decided that changing drinks would be a mistake, so they placed an order for two more pitchers of fresh margaritas. However, Holly suggested— and both women agreed—that there should be nine shots of tequila this time….three for each of them.

They had just toasted to the moon landing in the sixties when Bethany whistled. "Wow. Remember how I said I'd do Tuck-the-bartender for one-hundred K? Well, check out what just walked in the door. I think I'm going to melt off my seat."

Diana followed Bethany's gaze and moaned. "Oh, yeah. He is something. I'm thinking Navy. Maybe SEAL. Patrick would kick my ass for saying this, but Patrick who? That guy is totally yummy."

Facing the bar put Holly's back toward the door. She laughed at her tablemates. "Seriously? No guy looks that good." She turned in her seat and almost dropped her drink in her lap. She whipped back around. "Shit, shit, shit."

"What's wrong?" Bethany asked. She studied the guy closer. "Hey, Diana. Does that guy look about six-three?"

"I'd say so."

"Silver hair. Body to die for?"

"Yep," Diana said. "Can't see his eye color, but I'm guessing blue. What about you, Holly?"

"Don't call him over here," Holly said.

"Ben!" Bethany yelled. "Ben. Over here." She giggled. "He's coming this way. You were right, Holly. He's totally luscious."

Holly sprang from her chair and rushed to head him off. When she reached him, she threw her arms around his neck and pulled him close in hug.

"Please play along," she whispered in his ear. "It's a long story, and I don't have time to explain, but we're dating. Please."

Hot SEAL, Secret Service
A SEALs in Paradise Novella

As a Navy SEAL, and then as a Secret Service agent, Liam Ghost's best work is done out of the spotlight. When he's assigned to the Vice President's daughter, the magnetic pull between them leads to a hot, passionate affair. But the public attention on him, and on them, shines too bright a light and he backs away into shadows, leaving both of them pining for what they lost.

Liz Chanel is used to the being in the public eye. Through her formative years, her father served as state governor, senator and now vice president. When she falls for a member of her secret service detail, she feels every piece of her life is perfect...until her lover walks away. Even though she doesn't need the money, she jumps back into her modeling career in an effort forget Liam.

During an intense reelection campaign for her father, Liz is snatched off the runaway and held to force her father off the ticket.

Liam assembles a team of ex-SEALs to go get his woman back from the kidnappers, and maybe talk her back into his life.

"You know if this goes sideways and I get hurt, my wife is going to kill me. I promised this weekend would include nothing dangerous," said ex-Navy SEAL Nicholas "Falcon" Falcone. "And that I'd make it home by Christmas morning."

"Where did you say you were going?" asked Liam Ghost, aka Dagger One for this mission, aka ex-Secret Service and ex-SEAL.

"A SEAL convention."

The other three ex-SEALs seated on the floor in the back of the transport aircraft laughed along with Dagger One.

"At Christmas? She believed we hold conventions on Christmas Eve? And how did you explain why she couldn't come?" asked Levi Van der Hayden, aka Dutch.

"Didn't have to explain anything to Jen. She trusts me." He shook his head. "Actually, she knows me too well. She kissed me and told me she was going to buy herself a new Benz as a Christmas present from me while I was gone."

Dutch and Banger laughed.

Liam, who'd met Falcon's wife, nodded and asked, "Which one?"

"Who knows? She has expensive tastes so my money is on whichever model is the most expensive."

Liam chuckled. "In that case, my money's on a two-seater convertible."

"Five minutes to target," the pilot said into his mic.

"Man, I hate HALOs. I figured I was done with those when I left teams," said Heath "Banger" Diver.

HALO, otherwise known as high altitude-low opening jump, was one of the least favorite activities for most SEALs.

"Sorry, guys. It was this or a ten-mile hike in the snow with a steep, vertical ascent," Liam said.

"How good's the intel?" Dutch asked.

"Fairly solid. There are other teams being dispatched to other locations, but from the latest debrief, I think we've got the hot spot. Check your gear, gentlemen. Out the door in one minute. And before I forget, thanks for this. I know it's almost Christmas. You're doing me solid. I won't forget." Liam fist bumped each guy. "I promise you'll be home by Christmas Eve."

The plane's tail opened and the ramp slowly lowered. The team pushed up from the floor and shuffled toward the ramp.

"Good luck, guys," the pilot called out.

"Go time," Liam said. "See you on the ground."

Five bodies hurled from the plane.

A recent snowfall left fresh powder over harder, frozen ground providing a welcomed cushion to the landing. After quickly gathering their parachutes and stashing them under the limbs of snow-covered fir trees, each man took a snowboard from his backpack.

"Command. Dagger Team on location," Liam reported to the operations command center.

"Copy, Dagger One," Command responded. "Charlie Team and Beta Team hit dry holes. How copy?"

"Copy, Command. Dry Holes. What are you seeing on sat?"

"Eight heat signatures on the move. One stationary. No vehicle traffic. Copy?"

"Copy."

"VP scheduled to make statement in less than two hours. You have ninety minutes to secure site and locate hostage. Copy?"

"Copy. Ninety minutes."

"Dagger One, engage, but do not terminate. Copy?"

Liam gritted his teeth. Those bastards who held the love of his life deserved to die, preferably in some long, slow fashion.

"Dagger One. How copy?" Command repeated.

"Copy, Command. Engage, but do not kill the fuckers."

"Good luck," Command responded. "Out."

"Listen up," Liam said to his team. "The first two teams hit dry holes. Looks like we've got the prime target. SATCOM reports eight moving heat sigs, one stationary. We will assume that one to be the hostage. When we get within a mile of the cabin, Dutch and Banger break off and circle around to the east. Falcon, you and Mac go west. Once each side is secured, Dutch and Banger will move on to the south. Our orders are to capture tangos for interrogation and secure VIP package. Do not terminate tangos."

"You talking to us, Dagger One, or to yourself?" Dutch asked.

Liam grunted. "Good question, Dutch. I'll try to keep at least one alive to testify."

The five men bumped fists.

"Let's go," Liam said.

Hot SEAL, Sweet & Spicy
A SEALs in Paradise Novel

**Book TWO in the Grizzly Bitterroot Ranch Trilogy
Hot SEAL, Sweet and Spicy is a sweltering
standalone contemporary romance in the SEALs in
Paradise series.**

*She's hankering for some happiness. He's facing his fate
alone. Together, can they find forever on the menu?*

Addison Treadway needs time to heal. With her love-
less marriage finally demolished by her breast cancer
diagnosis, the talk-show host never expected to also
lose her job. And since her weekend as a bridesmaid is
her last before chemo, the thirty-three-year-old
resolves to put her perky girls to good use… and the
groom's hunky brother is the perfect choice to kiss
them goodbye.

Without orders to fulfill, Eli Miller feels aimless. With
the former Navy SEAL's duties now turned towards
the family farm, he's confused about what his future
holds. And before he can figure out his next move, he

finds the supposedly single woman he regretfully slept with at his brother's wedding is staying in his parents' apartment. Grateful to have acquaintances offer their home for her recovery from reconstructive surgery, Addison is floored when the sexy guy who ghosted her walks through the door. But when Eli uncovers the truth and sparks fly again, he starts cooking up something he's sure she's going to love.

Can they get past their awkward introduction and serve up a sizzling happily ever after?

To Eli, it felt like it was past time for him to pick up his share of the load.

Would he like being a cowboy again after being away for so many years? Would he miss the adrenaline rush of jumping from an airplane? Would he miss the ocean? The missions? His California friends? He had so many questions and so few answers. Only time would tell.

After dinner, he grabbed a Coke to go for caffeine and a couple of candy bars for sugar and got back on the road. At the rate he was going, he could be home around midnight and wake up in his own bed tomorrow. The idea spurred him to drive on.

When he reached the west entrance to Yellowstone National Park, he was glad he'd killed some time. Now early evening, there appeared to be more cars leaving than entering. July at Yellowstone was a traffic nightmare. Crazy to think he had to drive through this park to reach home, but straight through from the West entrance to the North entrance was the fastest route. At least at this hour, the traffic should be reasonable.

It was nearing ten-thirty when he rolled through the north exit of Yellowstone and into the city of Gardiner. Thirty minutes later, he turned off the highway and down the drive of Grizzly Bitterroot Ranch. A smile broke over his face, and a sense of peace filled his soul. He was home.

He parked his truck in the drive and slid out. His back cramped as he stretched his arms over his head and twisted from side to side. As he stretched, he studied the area. The lights were off at his parents' house. In the distance, he could see his brother and sister-in-law's new house. From where he stood, he couldn't see any lights there either. Cowboy Russ's house adjacent to the barn was dark. Ranch work started early, he remembered that, but he'd forgotten how early everyone turned out the lights.

When his parents built the newest, small feed storage barn, his mother had included a small apartment for her sister, if and when she came to visit, which wasn't often. The small, one-bedroom efficiency apartment was almost never occupied. His parents hadn't wanted to use it as a vacation rental because of its close proximity to the main house, so his coming home plan had included bunking there until he could get his house built, not that he had any idea of what he wanted to build or where. But there was no hurry.

Because their ranch was so far removed from the main road, the small barn apartment was rarely locked, and he doubted it'd be tonight. If it was, he knew where the key would be hidden. He'd surprise everyone at breakfast.

He stepped into the dark storage barn, stopping long enough to enjoy the aroma of hay, oats, horse liniment, and saddle leather. He smiled. Surprisingly, he had missed those scents.

The door that led into the hallway to the apartment was unlocked. He dropped his duffle bag in the laundry room and tried the apartment door. To his surprise, it was locked. He retrieved the key from the laundry room, unlocked the door and entered. Lights were on, which he found surprising, but maybe someone had left them on by accident. Or perhaps this was Zane's work. He had hinted to his brother that he could be home sooner than he'd planned. Inside the refrigerator was a six-pack of his favorite beer. Eli pulled one out, popped the top and took a long gulp. Bless his brother.

A woman's scream startled him and he dropped the beer onto the hardwood flooring. His head jerked toward the door of the bathroom and his mouth dropped open. Wrapped in an undersized towel, her left thigh exposed, and her hair wrapped in another towel stood the last woman who'd ripped out his heart and made him question love and marriage.

What the hell was Addison Treadway doing there?

SEALS IN PARADISE
EDITIONS

SEALs in Paradise: Favorite Drink Edition

Hot SEAL, Black Coffee, Cynthia D'Alba

Hot SEAL, Cold Beer, Cynthia D'Alba

Hot SEAL, S*x on the Beach, Delilah Devlin

Hot SEAL, Salty Dog, Elle James

Hot SEAL, Red Wine, Becca Jameson

Hot SEAL, Dirty Martini, Cat Johnson

Hot SEAL, Bourbon Neat, Parker Kincade

Hot SEAL, Single Malt, Kris Michaels

Hot SEAL, Rusty Nail, Teresa Reasor

SEALs in Paradise: Vacation/Relocation Edition

Hot SEAL, Alaskan Nights, Cynthia D'Alba

Hot SEAL, New Orleans Night, Delilah Devlin

Hot SEAL, Hawaiian Nights, Elle James

Hot SEAL, Australian Nights, Becca Jameson

Hot SEAL, Tijuana Nights, Cat Johnson

Hot SEAL, Vegas Nights, Parker Kincade

Hot SEAL, Savannah Nights, Kris Michaels

Hot SEAL, Roman Nights, Teresa Reasor

SEALs in Paradise: Wedding Edition

Hot SEAL, Bachelor Party, Elle James

Hot SEAL, Decoy Bride, Delilah Devlin

Hot SEAL, Runaway Bride, Cat Johnson

Hot SEAL, Cold Feet, Becca Jameson

Hot SEAL, Best Man, Parker Kincade

Hot SEAL, Confirmed Bachelor, Cynthia D'Alba

Hot SEAL, Taking The Plunge, Teresa Reasor

Hot SEAL, Undercover Groom, Maryann Jordan

SEALs in Paradise: Holiday Edition

Hot SEAL, Heartbreaker, Cat Johnson

Hot SEAL, Charmed, Parker Kincade

Hot SEAL, April's Fool, Becca Jameson

Hot SEAL, In His Memory, Delilah Devlin

Hot SEAL, A Forever Dad, Maryanne Jordon

Hot SEAL, Independence Day, Elle James

Hot SEAL, Sweet & Spicy, Cynthia D'Alba

Hot SEAL, Labor Day, Cynthia D'Alba

Hot SEAL, Midnight Magic, Teresa Reasor

Hot SEAL, Sinful Harvest, Parker Kincade

Hot SEAL, Silent Knight, Kris Michaels

Made in United States
Troutdale, OR
01/22/2024